A BAD GIRL WITH BENEFITS

"All right, soldier, you just gonna stand there and waste my time or do you want to get some ink?"

Kale put his head down and smirked as he started after her. He couldn't help liking her bad attitude. It was refreshing. She was feisty and quite possibly going to be a huge pain in the ass, but it turned him on. Oh, yes, this was going to be fun.

PRAISE FOR *THE VALENTINE'S ARRANGEMENT*

"Hot, sexy, and steamy. A very well-written story that flowed smoothly. The chemistry between Ronnie and Kale was palpable, and I was hooked from the first page until the last."

—Sydney Landon, *New York Times* bestselling author of *Weekends Required*

"Kelsie Leverich serves up fun, sexy and hot."

—Flirty and Dirty Book Blog

"I could feel the sizzle in the pages." —Into the Night Reviews

"Fast-paced and sexy as all get out." —Let's Get Romantical

continued . . .

"A great, fast, sexy story . . . it is a love story that was not all hearts and flowers and gushing and overkill." —Book Crush

"I read it in one sitting and loved every minute of it."
—Books She Reads

"Such a well-written, fun, emotional, spicy-hot story. . . . *The Valentine's Arrangement* is definitely a keeper." —Belle's Book Bag

"Mesmerizing. . . . I am looking forward to more of her writing."
—THESUBCLUBbooks

"A wonderful romance." —EbookObsessed

"Sexy read, loved every moment of this story." —Sensual Reads

"Emotional and worth every single minute." —Cocktails and Books

ALSO AVAILABLE FROM
KELSIE LEVERICH

Feel the Rush: A Hard Feelings Novel

Pretending She's His: A Hard Feelings Novella

THE VALENTINE'S ARRANGEMENT

A Hard Feelings Novel

KELSIE LEVERICH

A SIGNET ECLIPSE BOOK

SIGNET ECLIPSE
Published by the Penguin Group
Penguin Group (USA) LLC, 375 Hudson Street,
New York, New York 10014

USA | Canada | UK | Ireland | Australia | New Zealand | India | South Africa | China
penguin.com
A Penguin Random House Company

Published by Signet Eclipse, an imprint of New American Library, a division of Penguin Group (USA) LLC. Previously published in an InterMix edition.

First Signet Eclipse Printing, January 2014

LIBRARY OF CONGRESS CATALOGING-IN-PUBLICATION DATA:
Leverich, Kelsie.
The valentine's arrangement: a hard feelings novel/Kelsie Leverich.
p. cm.
ISBN 978-0-451-46665-5 (pbk.)
1. Women tattoo artists—Fiction. 2. Soldiers—Fiction. I. Title.
PS3612.E923455V35 2014
813'.6—dc23 2013032920

Printed in the United States of America
1 3 5 7 9 10 8 6 4 2

Set in New Caledonia
Designed by Spring Hoteling

PUBLISHER'S NOTE
This is a work of fiction. Names, characters, places, and incidents either are the product of the author's imagination or are used fictitiously, and any resemblance to actual persons, living or dead, business establishments, events, or locales is entirely coincidental.

To military spouses
because you get it.

ACKNOWLEDGEMENTS

There are so many I would love to thank. My family, my friends, my salon girls, my clients, my neighbor, my Keurig machine . . . the list goes on and on. Thank you, thank you, thank you!

I want to thank my husband, my hero, for supporting me while I chased this dream and for being my muse. I love you always.

I want to thank my mom, who is one of my very best friends, for always being there for me. And I want to thank my dad, who I pray never reads this book because that would just be awkward, for passing the love of reading and writing my way. I love you both.

I'm sending a big thank you to my smut-loving salon beauties, Stacey and Heather, for reading chapter by chapter and begging for more. Stacey, you encouraged me when I doubted myself, and you love my characters just as much as I do. Thanks, love. It means more to me than you will know. Heather, my sex-scene fiend, thank you for your smutty input and advice and for answering my calls when I was in a panic. Having the support and encouragement from you two made me believe in myself. I love you, girls, and if I haven't told you enough, thank you!

I want to thank all the amazing book bloggers and reviewers who took a chance on my book and supported me. Having a community that loves reading as much as I do support me on this crazy journey has been invaluable. You all are the best. Smooches!

And last but most certainly not least, I have to thank our service members and their families. The sacrifice both make for our country, for our freedom, is awe-inspiring. Being an Army wife, I have been fortunate enough to meet some of the best men I have ever known, and women that have become my lifelong friends, even if we don't talk every day anymore. Thank you.

THE VALENTINE'S ARRANGEMENT

ONE

Three more days and this hearts and flowers shit would be over. Three more days and the boxes of chocolates filled with things that should definitely not be paired with chocolate would be cleared from the shelves, the cheesy "Be Mine" balloons would deflate, and those damn stuffed gorillas, holding giant hearts, singing "Wild Thing," would be put to rest.

It was almost Valentine's Day in Watertown, New York, and the typical achromatic atmosphere at Fort Drum was replaced with shades of pinks and reds, complete with love banners and window decorations filled with hearts and chubby babies holding arrows. It was Ronnie Clark's personal week of hell.

Needless to say, Ronnie was not a fan of the lovey-dovey mushy shit; in fact, that was putting it graciously.

It was getting late, and Ronnie was listening to the soft tick of the second hand on her watch as she softly pressed the needle dipped in black ink into the hip of some lovesick barracks brat who had finally landed herself a private. You would think these girls would learn, right? Soldiers are lonely, and, yes, they look damn good in uniform, but the young, single ones are dangerous. They fall hard and fast and pull you in with their puppy-love eyes and promises of forever. These girls know it too; they are looking for it, and once they find it, it's a ring on the finger, a judge-officiated ceremony, and more often than not, it's matching ink declaring their love for each other. Blah blah blah . . .

"All right, Kara, I'm almost done with this locket. Are you sure you want me to put Craig's name under it? Names are not fun to cover up and I charge double to do it. I'm giving you your chance now," she said as she wiped the ink on Kara's hip, smearing it across the Celtic locket. Branding was not Ronnie's thing, but in this town, she was lucky if she went an entire workweek without getting stuck doing at least one.

"Yes, I'm sure." She narrowed her eyes at Ronnie before she turned them to her eager new husband, who was holding her hand.

"Don't say I didn't warn you," Ronnie mumbled under her breath. Oh how she wished she could just slap some sense into this girl. Sure, Craig was every shade of hot, and even Ronnie had an image of him without his uniform on begging to be brought to the forefront of her mind, but he was not tattoo worthy. No man was. No man was that damn permanent.

"Your six thirty sketch consult is here," Harold said, popping his tiny-ass head into Ronnie's room.

Ronnie slathered some ointment on top of the freshly branded flesh. "Tell him I will be there in a few. I'm just finishing up this girl's latest mistake."

"Ronnie!" Harold admonished, but he knew good and well that Ronnie said and did what she wanted and even he couldn't stop her. She was too good an artist to let go anyway. She was the best he had ever seen.

Ronnie lifted her head and raised her eyebrows at Harold, challenging him. He just shook his head and walked away.

"All right, keep it clean, but don't mess with it too much." She covered the girl's tattoo with a nonstick bandage and taped it down before turning and cleaning up.

"Harold will check you out." She stood from her chair and headed out of the room without as much as looking back behind her.

Most would call her rude, but she liked to think of it more as "real." She didn't sugarcoat anything and she wasn't going to pretend to like you if she didn't.

Ronnie sashayed to the front of the tattoo shop. She had one last client tonight and then she could slip off her heels and go home. Sure, she was going home to nothing, and not because her fiancé was still deployed and overseas, but because her fiancé was now an ex-fiancé and her solo living arrangement was now irreversible. Apparently her fiancé had a problem keeping it in his pants while he was gone, and his squad's female medic just so happened to be the lucky one to help him with his little, and she did mean little, dilemma. Okay, maybe she was being a smidge too hard on him . . . nah.

The shitty thing about it all—well, other than her fiancé sleeping around on her—was that she found out from someone else. His best friend, who just so happened to be deployed with him, called and told her what was going on. That was not a phone call that she wanted to get, let alone from someone other than the piece-of-shit cheater himself. When she confronted her fiancé about it he didn't even deny it, just acted like she should forget about it. He was halfway across the world, how could she possibly think he could wait that long? Fucking prick.

"Kale Emerson?" Ronnie said, scanning the waiting room. There were only two people there: one was Harold's intern, who was waiting to do his nightly bitch work, and the other one was a fuckingly handsome Captain America impersonator. He was tall, broad, and his well-defined arms were bulging through the thin material of his shirt. His sandy brown hair was cut short, barely enough on top to run your hands through, and of course he had to have blue eyes that seemed to grab onto hers with a force that held her captive. And for the first time in a long time, she felt vulnerable.

Kale Emerson turned around as a melodic voice sang out his name. Standing next to the front counter was a brunette bombshell in the sexiest purple heels he had ever seen on a woman's feet, making her damn near as tall as he was. Her legs went on forever and her almost black hair hung down past her shoulders and curled at the ends. Kale would like to say he saw her deep brown eyes first, but lying wasn't his strong suit and so help him if those lips weren't the first thing on that gorgeous face that caught his attention. They were plump, full, and cherry red and they parted into a smile when his eyes finally locked on hers.

Kale sauntered up to the counter and outstretched his hand. "Hi, I'm Kale. I have an appointment with Ronnie." The woman looked at his hand but didn't make a move to place hers in his.

"You're looking at her," she said bluntly.

"You're Ronnie?"

"Guilty. Come on back. We can talk in the design room."

Kale followed Ronnie through the narrow hallway, lined with framed drawings of cryptic angels and dragons, among other things. The entire place smelled like antiseptic cleaner, but Kale could still smell the hint of vanilla and musk that lingered in the air as Ronnie passed through. She was wearing a tight black shirt that dipped low into a V in the back, showcasing a delicate dream-catcher tattoo that started at the base of her neck and ended at the curve in her spine. The entire tattoo was done in shades of black; the only color was the turquoise beads dangling from the dream catcher. It was stunning; he had to refrain from reaching out and tracing it with his finger.

"Right in here." Ronnie stopped in front of a door leading to a large room and gestured for him to go on in.

"Ladies first," he said, reaching his hand out toward the open space in the door.

Ronnie's thick black eyebrows arched up and her full lips curved in a sexy-ass smirk. "I'm no lady," she said, then turned toward the room and glided in.

Kale followed her past the black sofa and flat-screen TV

to the back of the room where a large glass table with black leather desk chairs took up the back wall.

Ronnie sat down at the table, crossing her legs, and her shoe slipped off her heel causing it to dangle from her toes. Fuck, those heels were hot. Kale had been home from Iraq for all of six days. He had yet to sleep with a woman and this one sitting in front of him was becoming tempting.

Kale lived alone. He had no family to go home to, so coming back to Fort Drum for R & R was the only option. If he had his way, he would have just stayed with his platoon and continued to lead his troops, but he didn't have his way and it was mandatory he took his leave. He told his commander that he wanted to wait until after the holidays. Why should the men with families and kids have to miss Christmas if they didn't have to? No, Kale wouldn't be missing out on spending Christmas and New Year's with anyone: he wanted his soldiers to have that chance, so he opted to take his leave now instead. Six days down, eight more to go. Then it's back to the sandpit and Kale couldn't wait.

One perk about getting the hell out of that country was the women. It had been eight months since he had been in the States, and it had been eight months since he had had sex. Casual sex was Kale's forte. He didn't do relationships or commitment, just sex. Kale didn't have time to worry about putting someone else ahead of him; hell, he didn't even have time to put himself ahead of him. His soldiers came first, they always had. He loved his country and he loved his job, and a woman just didn't quite fit into that equation. No woman he had ever been with had been able to change his opinion either, but that didn't stop him from needing a woman to get underneath him from time to time. Now was one of those times and he wanted Ronnie to be that woman.

"All right, let's get down to business," Ronnie said, sliding a sketch pad in front of her from the middle of the table. "What do you have in mind?"

Her voice broke through his mental slush pile and brought him back. "I want a memorial tattoo."

"Okay."

Kale leaned back in his chair. "I want a poem, a soldier's prayer. I want it tattooed on my back, and I want it to look like my skin is ripping, revealing the words."

Ronnie wrote notes on her sketch pad.

"And I want the names of my fallen brothers to be after the prayer."

Ronnie looked up at Kale and an emotion flashed across her face that he didn't quite understand. It wasn't pity; was it awe?

"That's beautiful," she said quietly. Kale didn't know the first thing about this woman, but he gathered she didn't throw out compliments much. "How does the prayer go?" she asked, her eyes returning to her sketch pad as she prepared to write.

Kale slowly recited the prayer, his eyes locked on Ronnie as she wrote the words that told of courage and strength, of sacrifice and devotion. "And may my fallen brothers walk with you now, Lord. Amen."

Kale cleared his throat after he finished the names of his fallen soldiers, and rubbed his hand over the back of his head.

Their eyes met and Kale's mood shifted back. One look at her and he couldn't seem to think of anything but touching her. Yes, it apparently had been a long time because he felt like a twelve-year-old boy who just saw his first pair of boobs.

"I can have this ready for you tomorrow. When would you like to get started?" Ronnie asked as she closed her sketch pad and stood up. Kale stood up as well, his body leaning a little closer to her than he intended, and she took an immediate step back.

"Tomorrow will be fine." Kale shoved his hands in the pockets of his jeans to keep himself from grabbing her tiny waist and pulling her against him. That thought kept taunting him and he was damn ready to do it.

"Okay." She narrowed her big brown eyes at Kale, confusing the hell out of him. Ronnie walked back to the door and stopped, turning around with a hand on her hip. "You can stop fucking me in your mind now."

Kale's eyes came close to popping out of his head. "Excuse me?"

Ronnie rolled her eyes. "Let's get this straight, soldier. I'm not sleeping with you. You can get it out of your pretty little head, and I suggest you do so before I stick a needle in your skin." She turned back around, her sexy heels clicking out of the room.

Holy shit, he was sexy. And the way he was looking at her? He was threatening to make Ronnie come undone right there in the design room. She was used to having men gawk at her. She worked in a man's industry and had been subject to more than her fair share of pathetic one-liners and roaming eyeballs, but the way Kale looked at her was different; she didn't know what it was, but it was different. He was unashamed as he took her in, but he wasn't vulgar or offensive about it. He was just . . . hot. But he was a soldier and Ronnie sure as hell didn't do soldiers, not anymore.

"Since this is a large tattoo I need you to be my last appointment of the day. Can you be here tomorrow night at seven?" Ronnie asked as Kale finally emerged from the hallway.

"I will be here." He looked her in the eyes, unwavering and unaffected from the little threat she gave in the other room.

Before Kale walked around the reception desk, he stopped at the end of the hall and leaned in close to Ronnie. Her body jolted to attention the moment the heat from his breath hit her neck. She was about to spit out words to him that even her trailer-park, sailor-swearing momma would be embarrassed by when his hand touched the small of her back.

"For the record, sweetheart, I wasn't 'mind-fucking' you, but thank you for putting that image in my head." He pulled away, and his pretty-boy, clean-cut, "yes-sir" persona faltered a little bit. The corners of his mouth tilted just slightly into an imperative smile, but it didn't last long. "See you tomorrow night." His tone was now formal, like he hadn't just planted goose bumps along the side of her neck. Fuck, tomorrow was going to be interesting.

TWO

Kale pulled his truck into the local wing joint—for the third time since he'd been back—around five. His kitchen was lacking in the food department and with only a week left in the States, he didn't really see the point in grocery shopping. He would kill for a home-cooked meal like his grandma used to make, but he had the cooking skills of a ten-year-old. If you couldn't put it in the microwave, he didn't eat it. Needless to say, he had been eating most of his meals out.

The bar wasn't too busy and he snagged a seat in front of a flat-screen playing the Kings vs. the Flyers NHL game. He placed his order for an insanely large amount of wings and a beer.

"Well, if it isn't Sergeant First Class Emerson," a sweet, friendly voice said from behind him. He turned around to see Meagan, a girl he went out with a few times before he left for Iraq, standing close behind him.

He stood up and pulled her into a bear hug. He always liked Meagan. She was a sweet girl, never pushy or annoying, and she respected his relationship status. On top of that, she was a sexy blonde with full, soft curves and an overflowing handful of breasts. She looked like she had lost some weight while he was gone, but he wasn't going to say anything, he knew better than that. Besides, he thought he liked her a little bit thicker.

"Hey, Meg, how have you been?" he asked as he released her from his arms. She smiled shyly at him and took a small step back.

"Great, how about you? When did you get back?"

"A week ago."

"And you haven't called me?" She placed her hands on her hips in feigned annoyance.

"Sorry, Meg." He shrugged, genuinely sorry. He should have called her. He didn't know why he didn't even think about it. Maybe then his nights would have been filled with this woman warm in his bed. The idea would have usually had him asking her out right then and there, but something stopped him: the idea of possibly getting a certain walking art canvas in the form of a brunette bombshell with a bad attitude into his bed. You know what they say about the chase.

Meagan wrinkled her nose and laughed. "It's fine. I was just teasing you." She leaned into him, pressed a chaste kiss to his cheek, and placed a hand on his chest. She smelled so good and he could feel the warmth of her hand through his shirt. "My friend is waiting on me. I just wanted to say hi. It was so good to see you, Kale. I'm glad you're home. Be safe going back." She slid her hand down his chest. "We should get together while you're here."

She turned and as he watched her hips sway away, he thought they just might do that after all.

Kale walked into the tattoo shop, and sure enough, Ronnie was standing at the reception desk looking amazing. Any previous thought of calling Meagan tonight was washed from his mind. It didn't matter if it took him the rest of his leave to convince her, he was going to have this woman. She looked up at him and walked around the desk. Her hair was piled up on top of her head in a ball, and she was wearing a pair of jeans that looked like they were painted on her skin from hip to ankle—and those damn heels. They were black this time with studs along the sides, but they were just as sexy and did just as much to his imagination as the other ones did, if not more.

"Good, you're on time," she said without a hint of a smile. "Let's go."

She turned around and headed down the hallway. He just stood there like an idiot and watched her. Her hips rocked back and forth sweetly, and damn, if he thought those heels made her legs look amazing then he was going to have to check Webster's dictionary to find a word that described the way they made her ass look. He wasn't even sure such a word existed.

She turned around, her impassive expression turning irritated. "All right, soldier, you just gonna stand there and waste my time or do you want to get some ink?"

Kale put his head down and smirked as he started after

her. He couldn't help liking her bad attitude. It was refreshing. She was feisty and quite possibly going to be a huge pain in the ass, but it turned him on. Oh, yes, this was going to be fun.

Why did he have to come in here looking like a walking ad for Sexy 'R Us? Seriously, the pretty-boy thing didn't usually do it for Ronnie—actually it never did it for her—but Kale sure knew how to pull it off with just the right amount of bad-boy to make it tempt her. He had a beanie on his head and his face was scruffy today. When he slipped out of his coat a simple black shirt—which just so happened to be her favorite thing on a man—rested underneath. Nothing said hot like a nice, fitted, solid shirt clinging to a man's chest, hugging his thick arms. His jeans were worn and just the right amount of fitted to show off his massive thighs, but loose enough he didn't look like he needed to pair them with cowboy boots. Lord, help her when he took off his shirt.

Ronnie walked into her room, Kale following close behind her. She could feel his presence like a cloak of thick air surrounding her. She was sure that if she turned around he would run right into her. She stopped at the counter on the far wall and waited until his footsteps ceased before turning to face him. Just as she suspected, he was within arm's reach of her. Damn soldier.

"You can park it on that chair while I get set up," she said, turning back around so she was no longer facing him.

"Are you this nice to all your clients?" he asked sarcastically.

"Always," she replied with her own dose of venom behind her words.

After she set up her work area, she picked up the transfer paper of the tattoo she'd drawn up and turned back around to face Kale.

"Shirt off."

Kale lifted his shirt above his head and Ronnie made it a point not to look at his bare stomach. She could just imagine what it looked like and there was no way in hell she was going to let him see her look, no matter how badly she wanted to.

"All right, turn around," Ronnie said. Once Kale was positioned against the chair, his back facing Ronnie, she slowly and carefully placed the transfer paper on his warm skin and pressed down lightly. The muscles in his back flexed as her fingers brushed across his back.

"Take a look." She stepped back from the chair to allow Kale to get up and look in the mirror.

"Yeah, that looks great," he said, looking into the floor-length mirror from the small mirror he held in his hands.

"Good. Lie back down and get comfortable." She wanted his body lying down so she wouldn't be tempted to look at him—well, more tempted than she already was. Seeing him with his shirt off already had the idea of him removing the remainder of his clothing sticking out in her mind. Fuck. She wasn't supposed to be thinking about him like this.

"Bossy much?" Kale teased lightly, peeking over his shoulder at her as he leaned his chest against the back of the chair.

Ronnie just narrowed her eyes at him, not giving him the satisfaction of playing into his little game of bantering.

"Okay, okay." Kale sighed in defeat and leaned his forehead down to rest on his arms.

Ronnie ignored him as she put her gloves on and continued the final preparations. The sooner she got started the sooner she would finish. She already knew she was going to need a drink after this one.

"So how many tattoos does this one make for you?" Ronnie finally said, breaking the silence that stretched between them.

"First one."

"Tattoo virgin, huh? All right, soldier, let's see what you're made of." She splayed her left hand out on the bottom of his back and slowly lowered the tattoo gun to his skin.

The needle pierced his flesh, and she easily moved the gun across his static back.

Thirty minutes into the tattoo and she hadn't spoken another word to him. He lay still as a statue allowing her to do her work more easily. His head was still pressed against his arms so she couldn't see his eyes, but she could hear his calm even breaths, even over the buzzing from the tattoo gun.

"You hanging in there?" She looked at him out of the corner of her eye as she rubbed the ink away from the section of skin she was working on.

"Ah, she does have a heart after all," Kale said, shifting his head to the side to look at her, a dimple forming deep in his cheek as he smiled.

Yeah, she had a heart, just not one she was interested in sharing with anyone.

"Not a particularly large one, though." she said, smirking. "I just wanted to make sure you hadn't passed out on me."

"Not even close," he said. She could feel his eyes on her as she worked, and she silently wished she hadn't said anything to him. It was more distracting having him looking at her.

"So how long have you been doing tattoos?" Great, here comes the small talk. She really shouldn't have said anything to him.

Ronnie sighed. "Since I was twenty."

"So, that's been how long?"

"Didn't your momma ever tell you it's not polite to ask a lady her age?"

"My mother died when I was little, and besides, I thought you weren't a lady." He raised his sandy eyebrows at her and that fucking dimple made its reappearance.

Ronnie leaned back and looked at him. No pity lingered in her eyes; she wasn't offering him that by any means. Hell, her mom might as well have died when she was a baby too. Ronnie had been on her own since she was old enough to get herself on the school bus. No, nothing lingered in her eyes other than amusement. He was playing his cards though, that was for sure.

She softly wiped the angry flesh of his back with a clean, wet paper towel and returned the needle to his skin. "I've been tattooing since I dropped out of art school six years ago and followed my high school sweetheart from one post to another after he enlisted. I drove an hour each way to Austin, Texas, every single day for two years, interning for one of the best tattoo artists in the whole damn state. Fell in love with it and I've been doing it ever since."

"Hood, huh? I was stationed there a few years back."

And that was supposed to make her care, why?

"So this high school sweetheart who brought you to Drum, what does he do?" Kale's jaw clinched tightly as Ronnie ran the needle close to the side of his ribs. Men could be such pansies when she tattooed their ribs. She hadn't even batted an eye when she had hers done.

"Apparently he does any-fucking-thing with a vagina, and apparently it doesn't matter if she looks like a man either," Ronnie snapped, not really meaning to share her ex issues, it just sort of spewed out.

Ronnie looked at Kale out of the corner of her eye. His face was stolid as he watched her from the side.

"Care to elaborate?"

"Nope," she said, shooting her eyes toward him in a glare. His face didn't falter once. Ronnie rolled her eyes and shook her head as she leaned over his back, continued working, and sighed in defeat.

"My high school sweetheart turned into my fiancé. We moved to Drum about a year ago. He deployed to Afghanistan six months ago and has been sticking it to his squad's female medic for the last three. Now I'm just waiting for his sorry ass to get back so we can sell the house and I can get the hell out of this town." Her last few words were more to herself than to him.

Ronnie softly wiped Kale's back and leaned away. As she admired her work, Kale pushed away from the chair and angled his body toward her. Her stomach flinched when his blue eyes met hers, tearing into them with a fierceness that was raw and powerful. She wanted to look away, she needed to look away, but she couldn't.

"He committed himself to you and then he turned his back on you and your trust. He's not a man; he's a coward and a piece of shit."

Ronnie blinked and swallowed hard, not knowing what to say.

See, this was a prime example of why Kale didn't do relationships. They were hard enough as it was, and then throw in field time, late nights, and overseas deployments, and relationships went from hard to extremely difficult. He had seen the issues some of his men had had to work through, and it was no cakewalk. Spouses were left home, left taking care of the life that moves on while their soldiers were stuck living day by day in a hellhole. Soldiers were fighting for their country, their families, their brothers; and they were proud as shit to do it, but they did it all the while wishing like hell they were home with the people they love.

Then you had pieces of shit like Ronnie's ex, who took the pansy way out and crumbled when things got a little tough and expected it to be understandable. Bullshit. Once you commit to someone, you commit. You put that other person before yourself and you don't fuck it up.

That's why Kale kept it casual. Casual was simple. Sex was simple; it was just sex. He always made sure the women he spent his time with knew that's exactly what it was, just sex. Don't get him wrong, he treated them well; but he didn't want to lead them on, give them an idea of something more—Kale never wanted more.

Kale held Ronnie's gaze like it was the glue keeping her together. Her face softened and the hurt and betrayal she felt molded their way into her expression. He didn't say anything else; it wasn't his place and he could tell this wasn't a particular topic of conversation she was up for. Instead, he turned back around and draped his arms over the back of the chair, letting the silence fill the gaps of tension in the room.

Kale felt Ronnie shift closer to him and then he felt the thin latex of her gloves brush against his tender skin as her fingers grazed over his back. He wanted those gloves off her hands so he could feel the warmth of her skin running along his. He wanted her to touch him, really touch him.

"So how's it coming?" Kale asked, trying to shift the mood that seemed to be suffocating the room and shift his thoughts to ones that wouldn't make a tent form in his jeans.

"It's looking brilliant," she said, her voice full of satisfaction.

"I was told you were the best. I have to admit, I was a little surprised when I saw that the renowned Ronnie Clark was a woman."

"Why? You didn't think a woman could hold the title?"

"No. I was surprised because not one of the fuckers who sent me to you told me that the person who did their tattoos was saucy, outspoken, or stunning, let alone a woman—I'm pretty sure that little detail didn't just slip their mind."

Kale's buddies from his unit had some pretty impressive ink, and when they told him to go to see Ronnie Clark at No

Regrets tattoo shop, they knew good and well this woman would give Kale a run for his money; Kale knew now that those assholes had set him up.

"Flattery doesn't earn you any brownie points, soldier."

Kale chuckled quietly to himself. She wasn't taking his bait, not that he expected her to.

"I don't need brownie points." He could basically feel Ronnie's eyes rolling and he was enjoying ruffling her feathers.

"I'm sure you don't. I'm sure the girls just line up for the chance to jump into bed with the real-life Captain America."

"Captain America, huh?" Kale laughed.

"Don't flatter yourself. I'm more of a Hulk fan myself."

"So you like comic book superheroes?"

"I'm a female tattoo artist with a thing for fictional heroes, you caught me," she said insouciantly.

"That's kind of hot." Kale looked over his shoulder at her. A few strands of hair had fallen loose from the pile on top of her head and they were veiling her face, but he could clearly see the irritation pouted on her lips as she glared at him through the silky strands.

"Yeah, because that is exactly what I was going for when I picked up the nerd hobby of obsessing over comic books."

Kale laughed at her monotone responses. This woman was seriously a tough cookie to break. "Okay, so you're a sexy smart-ass who can tattoo better than any man around here, you have a soft spot for superheroes, and you like to wear sexy heels to work. What else?"

Ronnie lifted her eyes from his back and narrowed them at him. He had to suppress his laugh.

"You writing a fucking book?" she hissed.

"Nah, more like a list. Come on, what else you got for me?" he egged her on.

"I have a feeling I'm seriously going to regret this," she said, shaking her head back and forth as she returned the needle to Kale's back. He gave himself a proverbial pat on the back. He was wearing her down.

"I'm a secret *Twilight* fan," she mumbled.

Kale laughed hard, and Ronnie jerked her hand away from him. "Damn it, Emerson, hold the fuck still or I'm leaving this tattoo the way it is!"

Kale took in a deep breath. "I'm sorry. I wasn't expecting that from you . . . at all. Comic book superheroes, yes. I get it. They are badass, but sparkling vampires? I didn't see that coming."

"Yeah, and you'd better not repeat it," she said, a smile cracking on those full lips of hers.

"All right, your turn. What's your story?" Ronnie asked as she slipped her hand down Kale's side. Her eyes jerked toward her hand when she felt the smallest of trembles roll over him.

"What do you want to know?" His voice was low, confirming that the tremble Ronnie just felt wasn't from the tattoo.

"How long have you been in the Army?"

"Since I was nineteen."

Ronnie saw where this was going. "Ha ha, and how long has that been?"

"It'll be ten years in March," he said, his voice straining slightly when she pressed the needle over his spine. She lifted the needle and softly wiped the bleeding flesh. His muscles flexed under her touch and they were firm and thick. She needed him to keep talking, anything to distract her traitor mind from going where she didn't want it to go.

It was as if she spoke out loud because his body tensed and her fingers froze. She wasn't going to be able to get much work done with him responding to her every move like this.

"All right, I'm done," Ronnie said, pulling away and turning around toward the counter.

"You're finished? Seriously? It's been what, an hour?"

Ronnie slipped off her gloves after she discarded the used needle and turned around to face Kale. He had turned around and was sitting on the edge of the chair—his glorious, shirtless chest right in her line of vision.

"I'm not finished. I'm just done for the night. Come back tomorrow and we can finish it then." She handed him a mirror, and Kale stood up and faced his back toward the full-length mirror on the back of her door.

The entire front view of his body was facing her now, and she allowed her eyes to skim over the deep V of his hips and across his broad shoulders and down his thick arms and tight abs. She felt her face flush, and she turned away.

"Mic, I'm almost done here. You ready?" she hollered from her room, trying to distract herself.

"Damn, Ronnie. This looks amazing." Kale pulled the mirror down and handed it to her, then looked at his watch. "It's still pretty early; how about I buy you a drink?"

Ronnie sighed and closed her eyes. Apparently, she was going to have to fucking spell it out for him. "Look here, soldier, you know what I told you about mind-fucking me? Well, the same rule applies for attempting to fuck me."

"All right, sweetheart, it was just a drink," Kale said flatly, his eyes vexed.

"Yeah, well, I always go out for drinks with Mic on Friday nights anyway." Ronnie walked around Kale and placed a large bandage across his back. His body was still and rigid; it didn't react to her as it had moments ago, and she couldn't help thinking she pissed him off.

Kale slipped his shirt on over his head and picked his coat up off the chair. He smiled at her but the dimple in his cheek never formed. She risked her dignity and looked him in the eyes. Once again, they were unaffected. "See you tomorrow," he said, and then he turned from her and walked away.

"Two shots of Patrón and two Buds," Mic said to the bartender as Ronnie took a seat next to him at their usual dive bar in the building next to the tattoo shop. It was filled with smelly old men who had smoked their way past a lung transplant and had drunk so much they had long forgotten the meaning of sober. It was a rough crowd and an even rougher atmosphere, and it was blacklisted, which meant soldiers weren't allowed to come here courtesy of the post commander—just the way Ronnie liked it.

"All right, Angel, what's going on with you tonight? You

seem a little off." Yeah, he had no idea just how off Ronnie really was.

"Mic, you know I hate when you call me 'Angel.' I'm definitely no angel." Ronnie took the shot that the bartender set in front of her and tipped it back.

"Ah, you think a good angel would be hanging around my sorry ass? Nah, you're my little dark angel."

She laughed and took a drink of her beer. Mic was one of the tattoo artists she worked with at No Regrets, and he was probably her best friend there. Sure, he was fat and bald and old enough to be her dad, but he dished it out as much as Ronnie, and he could hold his own around her. She loved that about him.

"You gonna talk or am I going to have to buy the whole damn bottle of Patrón first?" Mic asked.

"What the fuck do you want me to say? I'm not off tonight, you're just delusional."

"Don't pull that shit with me, Ronnie. I know you better than that, and if I had to guess, your more stubborn than usual mood is because of that guy you were tattooing before we closed up. Am I right?" Mic lowered his head and looked up at Ronnie.

"Probably, considering all the guy did the whole time was attempt to flirt with me and ogle me like I was a piece of eye candy laid out there for his viewing pleasure," Ronnie hissed, even though the way he'd looked at her was anything but that. He'd looked at her like he wanted to devour her, and it was hot.

"Every man looks at you that way, Ronnie; fuck, I even look at you that way." Mic bounced his perverted-old-man eyebrows at her and she rolled her eyes. "You're used to that. Something tells me you liked it and that's why you're in extra-bitch-mode tonight."

Who was she kidding? She did like it. And if she was being honest, she liked looking at him too.

"I'm not having this conversation with you." Ronnie lifted her thick eyebrows and stared at Mic, trying to get him to back the fuck off.

"Nice try," Mic laughed. "It's time to get back on the horse, Angel. You've been single now for three months and haven't gone out with anyone. You're young and beautiful. You should be running circles around these fuckers. This soldier that has you all roused up may be able to show you a good time."

"Yeah, and that's all he's looking for. A little R&R sex, someone to ease his longing for a warm body, and someone to make him forget everything. Then he will be on his merry little way."

Mic finished his beer and slid it across the bar. "And what is wrong with that?"

Ronnie tipped her beer back, finishing hers as well. She raised her hand signaling for the bartender to bring them another round. She turned toward Mic who was staring at her, waiting for her to lash out. "You know what?" she said. "Nothing is wrong with that."

THREE

"You back for more?" Ronnie asked as Kale walked in the shop right on time the next night.

A smirk pulled up on Kale's lips and Ronnie was relieved he seemed to be in a good mood. She was afraid he would still be pissed after last night.

"Bring on the pain, sweetheart," Kale said, shrugging out of his coat. Like last night, he was in a solid T-shirt, but this one happened to be pale blue, almost gray, and it made the blue in his eyes that much more piercing—like he really needed something to make him more fucking attractive. He kept his eyes on her as she sized him up and that little cocky-ass smirk he kept on his face—probably because he knew she was watching—was really starting to piss her off. Fuck this.

She walked toward him, keeping her eyes on him and an impassive expression on her face. She passed him, walked to the door, and turned the lock.

Kale raised an eyebrow to her.

"Get your head out of your ass." She rolled her eyes. "It's

just us tonight and I won't be able to hear anyone come in while I'm working."

Kale lifted his hands as if in surrender, all the while trying to suppress a laugh. "I didn't say anything."

Ronnie's brown eyes smoldered, hot and angry, then turned into slits. "You didn't have to."

She strutted past him; his eyes were unashamed as they watched every move of every muscle in her body. She could still feel his eyes on her as she walked down the hall and she cursed her damn cheeks when she felt heat rise to the surface.

Kale followed her back to her room, and he was already taking his shirt off when she turned around to face him. He was purposefully trying to be sexy and, damn it, it was working.

"Go ahead and turn around and I'll line up the transfer."

He turned around slowly and she stepped toward him. The unfinished tattoo that spread across his lower back was already beautiful. She moved her appreciative gaze from his back to his narrow hips and down to his ass. She had the urge to run her nails down his back and hook her fingers into the waist of his jeans. Damn it. Instead, she rubbed a cotton pad soaked in rubbing alcohol across his skin. Goose bumps prickled on his arms and the span of his back widened as he sucked in a sharp breath.

"Shit, that's cold," he huffed.

"Don't be a pansy." She continued to wipe the cold, soaked pad over his back and enjoyed watching the muscles flex and tighten under her touch.

Another urge swept through her, and she found herself wanting to skim her mouth over his back and blow warm breath onto his skin, but she didn't. She placed the transfer paper onto his back and lined it up with the tattoo she had done yesterday. It wasn't nearly as sexy as her urges but the contact still had his body tensing. She pressed the paper to his skin and then slowly pulled it off.

As soon as she pulled away, Kale turned around and took a step toward her, closing the little distance that was between them.

Ronnie was tall. She was damn near five foot ten when she was wearing her four-inch heels, which she always was, and Kale still towered over her a good five inches. His head was tilted down toward her, and he was staring at her: at her eyes, then her mouth, then back to her eyes, and for a moment, she thought he was going to kiss her, or at least touch her, but he didn't.

She wanted him to touch her, but then at the same time she didn't. It was like being around him made her a freaking basket case of hormones.

"You have a personal space problem?" she asked, taking an infinitesimal step backward.

"Didn't think it was a problem," he said, his expression serious and intense. Fuck.

"Maybe not for you," she challenged, because it sure as hell was a problem for her. If she was going to keep in control of this little situation she seemed to have let herself get wrapped up in, then he was going to have to keep his distance. She already let herself think having a fling with him was okay, and she regretted thinking it the second Mic put the idea in her head. Ronnie was done with men and everything that came along with them: dates, sex, romance, and most definitely love. If only she could stand other females then maybe she could become a lesbian, but hell, she barely even liked to be friends with women so that idea was out.

She turned away from him to prep her work area because even the little annoying-ass angel propped up on her shoulder couldn't drown out the taunting words of the vixen devil that was perched on her other shoulder telling her to lean forward and run her hands down the length of his body. Ah, hell.

"So how long do you think it'll take you to finish tonight?" Kale asked as he sat down in the chair, but remained facing her. Her back was to him but he could tell she was still affected by him and he loved it. She was looking at him differently tonight. She was still snarky but her eyes were a little softer. She gave him an inch, and he was most definitely taking a mile.

"I'm almost done. I just need to add the names of the fallen soldiers and finish up some of the shading. I would say an hour." She sat down on her stool and rolled it toward him. "Turn around."

His eyes roamed over her one last time, allowing her to see him taking her in. He wanted her to know exactly what was running though his mind.

Her hair was down today, and he couldn't decide if he

liked it better that way or the way she had it last night. When it was down it brushed across the top of her breasts and gave him visions of grabbing handfuls of it in his hands, but when she wore it up he could see her long neck and delicate collarbone. It was a win either way.

She was wearing a gray-and-black-striped sweater that hung off her left shoulder and showed off the top of another tattoo, and he was sure it trailed down her entire arm. She had on another pair of pants that might as well have been painted on, but these were black cotton, and of course her fuck-me heels of the day were the same cherry red color as her lips.

After the full image of her was ingrained in his mind, he turned around and rested his arms on the back of the chair, keeping his face turned to the side, resting on his wrists, so he could watch her.

Ronnie quickly got to work on his back and the burning feeling of the needle tearing through his flesh was a dull distraction, but just barely.

Kale liked to watch her work. She bit the corner of her bottom lip and tilted her head as she concentrated. Her hands were gentle but precise and skilled as she carefully moved the gun elegantly across his back as if she were writing a sacred love letter. She licked her cherry lips every time she leaned back to admire her work, and she quietly hummed to herself in what seemed to be the most out-of-tune hum known to mankind. When she wasn't spitting fire, the hardness around her softened as if she was lost in her own little world and it sucked him in even more. He liked her feisty, but he could see the calm beneath the storm that consumed Ronnie, and he was determined to stay afloat until he reached it.

Oh hell, this was getting a little intense. She felt the heat from Kale's stare and she was damn lucky she was able to keep a steady hand. Ronnie didn't speak to him. Talking would slow her down and she needed the man out of her chair, out of the shop, and out of her mind. She already knew the latter was going to be fucking impossible. His eyes on her were like a drug that was quickly turning addictive and she was only three months sober from men, and it'd been six months since she had a hit to quell her body's need. Yes, getting him out of her mind was going to be difficult.

"You're awful quiet tonight." His voice rolled out of his mouth in a masculine purr that had her involuntarily pressing her thighs together.

"I just want to get this done with." She bit the words out to keep from screaming at the top of her lungs.

"Ronnie," he whispered, and the way his lips caressed her name sent a shiver down her spine, one that she couldn't ignore. One that didn't just create a path of goose bumps down the center of her body, but one that raised a soft tickle between her legs.

"I need a break; I'll be right back." She stood up and walked out of the room, needing to put some space between them. Ronnie headed for the back door that led to the alley where everyone at the shop took their hourly smoke breaks. She didn't stop to grab her coat from the design room and the cold winter air zapped her heated body, bringing her down from the mental high she seemed to be on. Ronnie just stood there, breathing the biting air into her lungs, allowing the night to lull her. She'd never had such raw sexual tension with someone before. Maybe it was because she knew she couldn't allow herself to give into him, or maybe it was because, for the first time since she was seventeen years old, she was allowing herself to think about being with another man.

Ronnie met Brandon, her fuck-face ex-fiancé, the end of her senior year of high school when he rode in on his motorcycle, whisking her away on the back of his bike with promises of forever, just like every other trailer park girl's fairy-tale ending. Too bad Brandon came from the same neighborhood as Ronnie and his juvenile record and GED weren't getting him into college anytime soon. Ronnie was barely able to pay her tuition at the community college for art classes.

Brandon was determined to make something of himself. He was determined to get the fuck out of that one-horse town and do something better with his life, to give Ronnie something better. She was swept away by the idea of it all, and she was in awe of Brandon's ambition. The Army did him good, too. Six years in and he was a sergeant fast-tracking his way up the promotion ladder, but his roots grabbed hold of him and swung him back down to be like every other piece-of-shit man that grew up in her neighborhood. He fucked around on her and who knows if it was even the first time. The Army had separated them a lot over the past six years.

Good, that was what she needed: to be reminded just

exactly why there was no way in hell she was getting involved with a soldier again, even if it was just for sex.

Ronnie took a deep breath and rubbed her hands up and down her arms to get the frozen blood in her veins moving again. She needed to stop being a fucking girl and get back in there to finish her job.

Ronnie pulled the heavy door open, her sweater covering her hand as she gripped the cold handle. The warm air of the shop stung her cheeks when she stepped inside. The moment the door shut behind her she was slammed against it, her back straightening against the pressure. Instantly a pair of hands gripped her waist, and at the same time, a pair of lips closed in on hers. Ronnie didn't have a second to process the chain of events that was taking place before her mind went into a dull fuzz as the blood left her brain and flowed quickly throughout her body, sending every nerve ending into a crazed sensation of complete pleasure.

Her eyes automatically closed, and her own hands reciprocated the touch and skimmed up the heavy bare chest that was pressing against her. She felt a shudder unfold beneath her fingertips, and it made her heart thud against her ribs. Kale was kissing her. No, he wasn't just kissing her, he was consuming her. He was touching her, and everything about the way his hands felt on her body was right, at least right now; and she decided to ignore the annoying angel still perched on her shoulder, giving in to the damn devil that was smirking with satisfaction.

Ronnie parted her lips and grazed her tongue across Kale's bottom lip, which caused the sexiest fucking groan to rumble in his throat. The noise had her arching her back, pressing her breasts hard against his chest as she wrapped her hands around the back of his neck, pulling him closer to her. His hands slid down her body and cupped her ass, lifting her up off the floor. Somewhere in the back of her mind, an inkling of a thought flickered, telling her that she shouldn't be doing this, but at that moment in time, she didn't give a shit. He was all hands and mouth and raw fucking desire; and right now, this was what she wanted. She wrapped her legs around his waist, and she could feel the thick bulge in his jeans, hard against the thin fabric of her leggings. Oh, it'd been a long fucking time since her body had felt the invasion of a man and she was trembling from the idea of it, from the idea of him inside her. She tightened her legs around his waist, pushing her hips into him so she could feel him more.

Kale swore under his breath and leaned into Ronnie, releasing his hands from under her and moving them to her breasts.

His weight was crushing her against the cold door, but she didn't care, she welcomed it. The feeling of this man devouring her was enough to make her forget her name, let alone the fact that she was hell-bent against doing this very thing.

His hands grasped her breasts with such force that it walked the line of painful; only she liked it and wanted more. She moaned in his mouth, closing her lips around his tongue and sucking hard. When she released it, she nipped his bottom lip.

Kale moved his mouth to her throat, right under her

chin. "You're killing me here, sweetheart," he breathed against her skin, sending warm pricks of pleasure cascading down her body until they settled low in her stomach.

She didn't respond; she couldn't. She just tilted her head back and allowed him to make her delirious with his mouth. He licked and sucked her tender skin until she was light-headed.

"Design room, now," she ordered, finally able to find her voice through the thick wall of seduction that was clouding her ability to remember how to speak.

Kale didn't say anything. Instead, he braced his hands on the door, one on each side of Ronnie's head. He pulled away from her neck and looked her hard in the eyes, looking for the slightest bit of doubt. He knew this woman reacted to him, but he sure as hell never would have imagined she would accept him so easily. When he raised his eyebrows at her, waiting for her to waver from her little command, she held his gaze with the most beautiful pair of brown eyes he had ever looked into.

When he was certain she wasn't going to jump from his arms changing her mind, he wrapped his arms around her and turned for the design room. She took that small slither of time he wasn't focused on her body and used it to run her teeth along his shoulder. Her hair bushed across his cheek and he could smell the sweet scent of her shampoo, but with the warmth of her body wrapped around his waist, he couldn't focus on anything other than the need to get her on the couch. He needed to touch her, to taste her.

Kale made his way into the design room, wading through the dark until his shins hit the couch. He lowered Ronnie down and didn't hesitate sliding on top of her. Her body was tiny underneath him regardless of her height, and she molded into the black leather as he pressed his lips to her shoulder.

He wanted to pull her clothes from her body and bury himself inside her until he passed out from pleasure, but he knew that he couldn't; not yet at least. But making her scream out his name, that he could do right now.

Kale's mouth traced over the side of her neck until it reached her ear. "I want to feel you," he whispered, cupping her through her thin cotton pants.

Her breath hitched and he took it as a yes. He brushed his fingers over her smooth stomach, reveling in the feel of her body trembling from his touch. He slipped his hand under the waist of her pants and inched his hand down until it reached the warmth he was craving. He cursed to himself when he felt the small amount of lace that was covering her. He had an urge to slip those damn pants off her long legs so he could look at the tempting material that was covering so very little of her, but he knew he was bound to lose his control if his eyes were involved.

His thumb softly skimmed over the lace and he could feel how ready she was for him. He smiled against her neck, loving the way her body responded to him. He pushed the lace aside and gently slid his fingers inside her. He sucked in a breath when she instantly tightened around him. Damn, she felt good. It had been way too long since he had felt a woman's body like this.

Ronnie's head fell back and her body rocked against his hand as he rotated his fingers, finding the exact spot that seemed to drive her senseless. He stayed there, stroking her with the tips of his fingers, begging her to quiver beneath him.

Little breathy moans escaped her lips, and with each stroke, Kale's chest tightened and his resolve started slipping further and further away.

"I need to taste you, and I need to do it now," Kale said, lifting his head from Ronnie's neck so he could look her in the eyes, all the while keeping his fingers in place.

He drove farther inside her and rubbed the heel of his palm against her. She moaned again, only it wasn't breathy and quiet this time and he knew she was getting close. He slowed his fingers, keeping his eyes on her, waiting for permission.

"Please," she whispered.

"Please what, baby?"

"Yes. Now, please," she begged, and he loved that he made this hard-ass woman beg for him.

Wasting no more time, he withdrew his fingers and trailed his hands down her legs until they reached her ankles.

"I hate to see these go," he said, slipping her cherry red heels from her feet. He lifted her foot to his mouth and licked a path from the inside of her heel to her toe. She giggled softly and it was a sweet sound, one he very much liked making her do, and one he was sure she didn't do often.

He put her foot down and did the same to the other until both heels were off and he was slipping her pants from her hips.

"Maybe I can get you to keep those shoes on for me sometime," he said with a smirk planted firmly on his face.

Ronnie glowered at him, her eyes squinting into slits, causing Kale to laugh. "Okay, okay," he said, although he was damn sure gonna try. Those heels were too hot not to see them paired with her naked body. The thought almost made him put them back on her, almost, but the need to get his mouth on her won out.

He pulled the skintight fabric from her body and looked at her, using the light from the hallway to aid his eyes, and fuck, those legs were sexy before, but seeing them now, bare and beautiful, had him second-guessing his imagination because this was even better than he thought. They were long, delicate, and creamy. The idea of them wrapped around his body again came to the forefront of his mind, but there would be time for that later.

A tattoo on the side of her rib cage peeked out of the bottom of her sweater and continued all the way down her hip and thigh. He wished he had taken a second to turn the lights on so he could admire the art covering her beautiful body.

"Kale," Ronnie sighed, causing him to break his gaze from her legs. The sound of his name coming out of her mouth in a plea was the sexiest sound he had ever heard. Everything about this woman was causing insistent needs to radiate throughout his body, and it was hard for him to stay on track, but he was going to if it killed him.

He ran his hands down her legs, stopping at her knees to spread her open so he could settle between them. Yes, the barely there lace that was covering her was doing just as he expected, making his control falter. It'd been so long since he had been with a woman; the need was almost painful, especially with the beauty that was Ronnie spread open before him. But this wasn't just about him; his need to do things to her body and make her shudder was even more essential.

Kale hooked his fingers on the thin straps that were covering her hips and he eagerly pulled the damn thing off.

The sight of her damn near knocked him senseless. She was beautiful.

His mouth was on her in the very next moment. He was relentless with her, stroking her with his tongue, riding it out with her until she was just about there and then pulling back, bringing her down slowly so he could repeat it all over again.

"Kale . . . fuck . . . ugh, don't stop . . ." Ronnie bit the words out as if each syllable was a strain. Her body was shaking. He knew he had pushed her long enough, and he was dying to have her come undone against his mouth. He slid a finger inside her, finding that same spot that he knew would send her over the edge as he swirled his tongue over her clit.

Her hands flew to his head and her nails dug into his scalp as she trembled against him and screamed out. It was the most perfect moment he had had since he left for the war. Feeling this woman lose herself with him was exactly what he needed.

Holy fucking . . . that was the single most amazing orgasm she had ever experienced. The urgent way Kale devoured her was mind-blowing. It was as if he was starving for her. Brandon never touched her like that. He never made her feel like if he wasn't with her, he was going to explode. He never made her feel like he couldn't get enough of her. He sure as fuck never spent the time to make her world spin on its axis. But Kale . . . he was . . . he did . . . fuck, he was good; and she had only experienced his mouth. What would it be like if he used his body, if he pressed himself inside her? She needed it. The thought made her squirm, and a moan rolled out of her mouth.

"Damn, sweetheart," Kale said, kissing his way up her stomach, pushing her sweater up with his hands. "You're still trembling." He latched onto her waist, slipping his arm underneath her, clinging to her and pulling her to his chest as he lay down next to her. This simple touch, this simple movement made her body freeze like it was stunned with glacier water.

"Don't," she protested, begging her limbs to defrost so she could push him away.

"What?" Kale's voice was full of concern; it made her stomach drop.

"Don't hold me. This isn't . . . just . . . don't." She finally found some muscles that seemed to be in working form, and she moved her body until she was pressed into the corner of the couch.

"I don't understand." Kale sat up, giving her the space that she so desperately needed. "I thought you were enjoying yourself. I thought you wanted this." There was an edge to his voice, one that she didn't understand.

"I—"

"Ronnie?" A voice carried through from the other room.

"Fuck. Jordan—" Ronnie whispered urgently.

Kale leapt from the couch, shielding Ronnie with his body. He leaned down, picked her clothes up from the floor, and handed them to her.

"Who? I thought you locked the door?" Kale was firm and unmoving in front of her as she quickly slipped on her pants.

"I did, but that's the boss's daughter. She has a key." Ronnie stood up and stepped into her heels.

Kale's eyes lowered and his lips turned up on the corners. "Yes, I do prefer those on."

"Watch it, soldier."

"Ronnie, are you still here?" Jordan called out, her voice closer to the design room now, and Ronnie was grateful for Jordan's not so perfect timing.

"Yes!" Ronnie hurried past Kale to the hallway, flipping the light on in the design room before damn near running straight into Jordan.

"There you are. What are you doing? Didn't you hear me?" Jordan asked, jumping a step back.

"Fuck, Jordan, you scared the shit out of me. I was reprinting my design. I thought you were coming by at ten."

"It is ten," Jordan said, looking over Ronnie's shoulder to what she assumed was her freshly aroused Captain America impersonator. Jordan's barely there blond eyebrows reached her hairline as she looked from Kale to Ronnie.

"I'm almost done." Ronnie met Jordan's eyes like a mountain lion staring down its prey. If Jordan didn't back the fuck off and drop what Ronnie knew she was about to say, then Ronnie would attack. She was not in the mood for this.

"Okaay." Jordan dragged the word out and followed Ronnie back to her room. Jordan was one of the only females Ronnie could actually stand to be around. Hell, she was the only female friend Ronnie had for that matter. She was a couple years younger than Ronnie but she was cool as shit. She didn't pry or gossip or whine like most women. She was real. She was simple; no tattoos, no piercings, her hair was its natural dishwater blond and her face was rarely covered in makeup other than mascara on her crazy-long lashes. She didn't need any of that shit anyway; she was a natural beauty. Other than the fact she was itty-bitty like her father, you would have never guessed that Harold, the owner of the tattoo shop, was her dad.

"How much longer are you gonna be? I put my heels on just for you, and I'm ready to shake my ass. Plus I've got Cameron all good and liquored up, so he is ready to show us a good time." Jordan walked in and planted her butt down in one of the chairs in Ronnie's room.

"Who's Cameron?" Kale asked, walking in the room after Jordan. There was a slightly territorial tone to his voice that made Ronnie's heart speed up.

"None of your business," Ronnie barked, narrowing her eyes at Kale. Who the fuck did he think he was butting into her personal conversation? Just because they had a moment—okay, a very hot and sexy moment—in the design room, didn't mean he could spout out questions whenever he wanted.

"My sexy-as-hell husband, that's who!" Jordan squealed. Yes, she actually squealed, and Ronnie cringed.

"Newlyweds," Ronnie said to Kale, feeling the need to explain her friend's sudden outburst of giddy girliness.

"Ah, enough said," Kale laughed, and Ronnie couldn't help smiling. Kale resumed his position against the chair as Ronnie slipped on a clean pair of gloves.

"But seriously, how much longer? I'm sure there's going to be a mile-long line to get into Club Zero if we get there past eleven, and it's freezing outside."

"Okay, Jordy, get the fuck out and let me finish then," Ronnie lashed.

Jordan stood up and grinned sweetly at Ronnie, gaining an eye roll from her before she turned and walked out.

"Club Zero, huh?" Kale asked, turning his head slightly to peer at Ronnie from the side.

"Yep," was the only response she gave him. He wanted to bring up whatever it was that happened in the other room. He wanted to know what was going on in that crazy mind of hers. Just when he thought he had cracked the surface, she revealed a completely new layer.

Ronnie didn't speak to him, she just pressed the needle to his flesh and worked in silence, and he didn't press her either.

When she was finished, she wiped his back softly and rubbed a thick ointment across his entire back. Her light touch on his raw, angry skin walked the line of pure bliss and pure hell at the same time.

Kale turned toward her when her hands left his body and the lustrous expression that was carved into her face was new, and it made her look even more beautiful. She was completely glowing with satisfaction and joy.

"All right, soldier. Take a look," Ronnie said, handing him a mirror.

Kale lifted the hand mirror so he could see the reflection of his back in the full-length mirror behind her door.

"Wow," was all he could say.

"Pretty fucking amazing, huh?" Ronnie managed to ask through her smile, one that reached all the way to her eyes.

"For lack of a better word, yeah." Kale locked eyes with her and watched as she carefully covered up the layer that she let slip through.

He lifted the mirror back up and studied the art that this woman had embedded in his flesh. The words of the poem that meant so much to Kale on so many different levels seemed to be buried deep in his skin, straining to be ripped to the surface. It was compelling. It was sad and inspiring and disturbingly beautiful. Just like Ronnie.

FOUR

"So, who was the hottie?" Jordan asked as Ronnie slid into the cab.

"Just some soldier home on R and R. Sergeant First Class Emerson." She lowered her voice a few octaves trying to imitate a mocking man's voice.

Cameron turned around in his seat next to the balding, overweight cabdriver. "Sergeant Emerson? He's a kick-ass master gunner. He's in Bravo Company, I think."

"You know him?" Ronnie asked, and she didn't know why she was suddenly interested in what Jordan's new husband had to say.

"No, but I've heard of him. Amazing leader; people either love him or hate him, though. He tells it how it is and doesn't give a shit who you are. If you're wrong, you're wrong, wouldn't matter if you were the fucking president of the United States. He takes damn good care of his men too. My buddy Rodrigo was in his platoon back at Hood."

That was unexpected. She would have never guessed that clean-cut, not-a-single-eyebrow-or-hair-out-of-place Kale

Emerson was one to ruffle the feathers in his chain of command. The fact that the real-life Captain America wasn't as by-the-book as she had first thought kind of turned her on.

The cab pulled up in front of the club a little before eleven, and, just as Jordan had predicted, there was a line waiting to get in. No way in hell was Ronnie standing outside in this damn weather waiting to get into a club. Fuck, no. She would rather just go home.

"Pull up a little closer to the door," Ronnie told the driver.

He did as she said, and Ronnie smiled when she saw the short, stocky Mexican man checking IDs. "Let us out here."

Ronnie opened the door, and the freezing night air slammed into her. She grabbed ahold of Jordan's hand and pulled her and Cameron through the line of people who were cursing at them as they made their way to the front.

"Well, Ronnie Clark. How are ya?" The bouncer smiled a full, pearly white, toothy grin. Ronnie tattooed him a few months back after his wife had their first baby. It was one of her favorites, a portrait of his wife holding their newborn son.

"I would be a lot better if I was out of this damn cold-ass weather, José," she said as she took his hand and he hugged her from the side.

"Go on in," he said with a smile, letting Ronnie and her friends pass by.

"Thanks, José," she hollered back to him.

"Anytime."

"Let me guess: a client of yours?" Jordan asked as they got their hands stamped inside the door.

"Yep."

She nudged Ronnie with her shoulder. "You come in handy—you know that?"

Ronnie rolled her eyes and made a beeline for the bar. After the evening she just had, she was all for drowning herself in a bottle of self-pity, preferably in the form of Patrón.

Ronnie slammed back a shot then picked up her beer and found Jordan who was perched on a barstool. "Where's Cameron?" she asked, taking a seat next to her at the table that ran along the perimeter of the dance floor.

"He just went to get us some drinks. He's grabbing you a beer too," she said, eyeing the one in Ronnie's hand.

"Good." Ronnie tipped back the bottle and finished its contents in a few long swigs. She set the now-empty bottle down. "I need another one." She smiled at Jordan who just shook her head.

"It's gonna be one of those nights, huh?"

"When isn't it one of those nights?"

Jordan laughed. "Touché."

Cameron came back with three beers in hand and passed two to the girls. Ronnie took a drink then stood up; the blood rushing through her veins numbed her body slightly, and she grinned at the sensation.

"What are you doing?" Jordan giggled as Cameron nuzzled her neck.

"I'm going to dance," Ronnie said. Then she sashayed onto the dance floor.

The music was a mixture of pop techno remixes and rap. She didn't care what they were playing as long as the music didn't stop. Getting lost in music held second to Ronnie getting lost in her art; it took her somewhere where she didn't have to think about anything. Add liquor to the equation and she was good to go.

Her body moved to the beat and she let her mind slip away. She released all the conflicting thoughts she had about Kale and what she let him do to her in the design room, and all thoughts about letting him do it again. She just moved. It was cathartic.

After a few songs, her hair started clinging to the base of her neck and the arches of her feet started to scream, but she didn't give a damn.

"Well, hello," Jordan said, slipping in next to Ronnie.

Ronnie spun around to face Jordan. "Hello yourself."

She tried hard to hold in the laugh that was busting at the seams when she saw a not horrible-looking, but scrawny, guy attempting to dance behind Jordan. He kept inching closer and just before he grabbed ahold of Jordan's waist to dance with her, Ronnie grabbed her hand and pulled her away.

"Do you see a 'take one' sign plastered on her ass? I didn't think so. Ask a woman to dance before you just put your damn hands on her. And no, she doesn't want to fucking dance with you." The words whipped out of Ronnie's mouth, leaving the young guy bloodred in the face as he turned and hurried off the dance floor.

Jordan rolled with laughter. "See, this is why Cameron never cares if I go out with you. Hell, I think guys are more afraid of you than they would be of him anyway."

"Fucking soldiers," she barked.

"How do you know he was a soldier?"

"He had an infantry tattoo on his forearm."

"Leave it to you to pick out tattoos."

Ronnie just smiled.

After brushing off a few more douche bags that tried to dance with her and Jordan, she grabbed Jordy by the hand and stomped off the dance floor.

"Can't these guys get a fucking clue and leave us the fuck alone? For fuck's sake." She plopped down on the barstool next to Cameron where he sat holding down the fort.

He laughed and pulled Jordan onto his lap. "Can you say fuck any more in one sentence?"

"Yes, I fucking can," Ronnie spat before taking a drink of her now-warm beer. "I'm going to get another drink, want anything?"

"Nope, I'm good," Jordan said, grabbing Cameron's hand and pulling him up from his seat and onto the dance floor.

Ronnie laughed aloud at her friend. Jordy was basically having sex with Cameron right then and there on the dance floor. She really did love that girl.

Ronnie squeezed her way to the bar, sending a few "go-to-hell" looks at some drooling guys as she passed them. Luckily, a heavyset redhead stood up from her barstool at the same time Ronnie reached the bar.

"Can I snag your seat?" Ronnie asked the woman.

"It's all yours," she said before she walked away. Thank God, because Ronnie's feet needed an intermission.

"What's your poison?" a voice said close to her ear, making her already heated skin even stickier from the warmth of his breath. She turned around on her stool to see a very sexy

Sergeant First Class Emerson standing behind her with a scruffy smile on his face. He was in the same worn jeans as before but he had changed his shirt to a snug-fitting, black button-down with the sleeves rolled up to his elbows. He was such a pretty boy.

She forced herself to tear her eyes away from him to keep from staring at his chest and the way his damn preppy shirt pulled across it. "Patrón."

"Two shots of Patrón," he told the skanky bartender in a tube top and a pair of jeans that was unfortunately close to showing off her lady goods. The bartender smiled and was all too happy to tend to him.

She leaned seductively over the bar as she slid the shots to Kale. "Here ya go." She winked.

"Seriously?" Ronnie huffed, raising her eyebrows at the bartender before grabbing her shot and tossing it back. The bartender looked from Ronnie to Kale—who was more than likely mind-fucking Ronnie at that very moment by the way he was looking at her—before pouting her way on to the next customer.

"What are you doing here?" Ronnie asked, peeling the paper off her beer bottle.

"Turns out, this tattoo I got on my back stings like hell, figured I could use a drink to dull the pain a little." He leaned in close to her. "Plus the idea of watching you dance held its own persuasion."

A wanton shiver slithered down Ronnie's spine and she hoped like hell Kale didn't notice. "So what, now you want small talk?"

"Small talk, no talk, I don't care," he said, motioning with his hand for the bartender to bring them another round. Great, Ronnie was going to have to witness that bimbo make a fool of herself again.

Kale slowly and deliberately stepped closer to her. She could almost feel him against her side. "Dance with me."

"I'm not dancing with you."

"Dance with me," he said again, offering his hand to her.

"Look, soldier, I don't know who the hell you think you are, but you can't just order me around."

He leaned down and ran his nose up the side of her neck and she stilled. "Well, as of right now, I'm finding it extremely difficult not to push you up against this bar and put my mouth on your body; you're tempting me and I just might do it. So, you can either dance with me and let me attempt to get the image of you squirming beneath me out of my head, or you can leave with me now and we can replay that image in real time."

Ronnie's formerly clear mind started swimming with the memory of his body crushing her against the door eagerly kissing her, and the feel of his body pressing her into the couch, and then the feel of his mouth, oh his fucking mouth on her . . . damn it.

"And you think I'll just leave with you, why?" she asked, pulling her mind back to the present where Kale was leaning dangerously close to her. She could smell the faint scent of soap on his skin.

"Because I know you enjoyed the little taste of me that you had back at the shop, and God knows I enjoyed tasting you." He smirked. "And because I can see it in your eyes now. Dance with me."

The bartender slid the shots in front of them, thankfully without attempting to flirt, and Ronnie once again tilted the shot back, letting the clear smooth liquid run down her throat.

She stood up and grabbed his hand, causing that fucking dimple to drill deep into his cheek. "You'd better not make me regret this," she said, leading the way to the dance floor.

The second Ronnie stepped onto the dance floor Kale jerked back on her hand, spinning her around until she was pressed against him. He slid his hands down her arms and then latched onto her waist. His hands were large on her hips and they held her like he was afraid she was going to run for the hills. He slid his thick thigh in between her legs and started moving them to the music.

She wasn't going to lie to herself and pretend he wasn't turning her on with every single touch, but was she going to pretend to Kale . . . absolutely. He already was cocky with the way he looked at her, she didn't need to fuel him further; but damn it, his hands felt good on her body. She had to strain from shuddering when he ran a hand up her spine and grabbed ahold of the back of her neck.

She didn't dare look him in the eyes because she was sure that "fuck me" eyes would be staring back at her, and she was starting to second-guess her willpower to say no.

And then, he just had to go and slip his fingers through the hair at the base of her neck to pull her head back . . . damn it. Of course, that was followed by him leaning down and running his mouth up her neck from the dip in her collarbone to her chin. She moaned, fucking hell she moaned.

She felt Kale's lips tighten into a smile on her skin. "You like my mouth on you?" he whispered against her skin, and even with the heat from the crammed bodies surrounding her and the sweat trickling down the back of her neck, she got chills.

Kale spun her around so her back was pressed against his chest and he wrapped his hands around her stomach. He pulled her tight against him and slid his fingers perilously down her stomach.

Ronnie could play this game too. She lifted the hair off her neck and swirled her hips, pushing her ass into his groin as she moved with him to the music. She felt his body rise against the small of her back and she smiled to herself.

This woman was good; she knew exactly what she was doing to him, and he liked it. He wanted her to push his buttons; he wanted her to want this. Hell, after the way she ended things back in the design room he was glad she was letting him touch her at all.

Kale took the opportunity that was in front of him and leaned forward. He pressed his mouth to the back of Ronnie's neck, causing her to jerk against him. He smiled again, loving how easily he affected her, and then he slipped his tongue out and licked the moisture that was accumulating under her hairline.

A shudder ran through Ronnie and Kale tightened his

hands on her stomach to keep her still. "I knew you liked my mouth on you," he whispered in her ear.

Ronnie spun around to face him, placing her hands on his chest. "Did I ever say that I didn't?" she challenged, and Kale gladly accepted. He buried his nose in the curve of her shoulder and she tilted her head to the side offering him better access. He sucked her collarbone and skimmed his teeth over her skin, nipping her shoulder. She tasted good—sweet and hot.

"Hey, Ronnie, uh, I'm sorry to interrupt." The girl from earlier, Jordan, was standing behind Ronnie, trying hard to suppress her grin as she looked at Kale. Yeah, this girl sure had a way of interrupting him. "But we have to go."

Ronnie stepped out of Kale's arms and turned to face her friend. "What? What's wrong?"

"Cameron had one too many drinks tonight. I shouldn't have gotten him drunk before we left the house, but you know how he hates to dance . . ."

"Jordan . . ." Ronnie said, halting Jordan's rambling.

"He's a stumbling mess and he just spilled his beer all over one of the bouncers. They're kicking him out. They have him up front. I'm sorry, but we need to go."

"All right, I'll meet you outside; I have to pay my tab." Ronnie turned and walked off the dance floor and Kale hurried after her.

"I can take you home," he said, stepping up beside her.

She sent him a malicious look and shook her head. "No."

Okay. He wasn't going to press his luck with that one. "You have a date for Valentine's Day tomorrow?" he asked as they reached the bar.

Ronnie narrowed her eyes at him and laughed. "Hell, no."

"What?" Kale didn't understand what was so funny to her.

"Valentine's Day is a joke. I hate it."

"You hate Valentine's Day? Isn't that supposed to be a woman's favorite holiday?"

"Do I seem like your typical woman?" she asked. No, she definitely wasn't like most women, and that's exactly what he liked about her.

"I hate everything about it," she said. "The candy, the cards, the flowers, and the fucking balloons. Oh, and the chocolate. Don't even getting me started with the chocolate. Who ruins a perfectly good piece of chocolate by putting fake fruit-flavored goo inside? No, the only date I'll be having is with my couch, a six-pack, and Freddie Krueger."

"Come on. What's one little date going to hurt?" Kale pulled out his pretty-please smile and handed the bartender a fifty as she came with Ronnie's receipt.

Ronnie's eyes disappeared beneath her lashes, glaring, as she ripped the bill out of the woman's hand and shoved it against Kale's chest.

"I wanted to pay for—"

"I don't date either, and that would include you paying my tab," Ronnie said, handing the bartender her card. Kale looked at her expectantly, waiting for her to explain. He'd never met a woman that turned away free drinks.

"I'm done with that shit. I'm done with dating and relationships and everything that comes along with them," she said. Ronnie's phone lit up inside her purse and she pulled it out and put it to her ear. "Jordan, I'm hurrying," she said as she answered. "What . . . are you fucking kidding me . . . Jordan, it's fine, you're not paying for my cab . . . no you're not, I've got it . . . yeah. . . . all right, 'bye."

"What was that about?" Kale finally asked when Ronnie got off the phone.

"Cameron's dumb-ass was running his mouth outside and the club threatened to call the cops, so they left."

"They just left you here?" Kale's jaw clenched as he tried not to get pissed off, but who in the hell leaves a woman at a club by herself? That dumb-ass should have better sense to take care of the women he is with instead of getting wasted. Kale's hands tightened into fists just thinking about it.

"It's no big deal. I'm a big girl. I can get my own cab." Ronnie was signing her receipt so Kale couldn't see her eyes to know whether or not she was upset about her friends bailing on her. Even though it pissed Kale off, he didn't think it bothered Ronnie all that much.

"I'm taking you home," he said, leaving no room for arguing.

"You're not taking me home. Fuck, what is with you and thinking you can order me around? I'm not one of your soldiers who are going to stand at attention and say 'Yes, sir.'" She turned on her heels and headed for the front of the club.

Kale followed close behind her, trying to decide whether or not he should reach out for her. She had the mood swings of a woman diagnosed with bipolar disorder who was on the rag, and since he was fond of his limbs, he decided against it.

Finally, Kale stepped around her when she reached the door that led outside. "Look, I'm not trying to order you around . . . and I get that you can handle yourself, but I would like to make sure you get home all right. Is that really too much to ask?" Kale knew he was probably pushing her too far, especially since her face was wound up so tight he could barely see the whites in her eyes; but Kale never left a woman on her own at night and he wasn't going to start now. He didn't care if he had to follow the damn cab to make sure she arrived home okay, he would do it.

"You are seriously the biggest pain in the ass—you know that?" Ronnie said, slamming her palm onto Kale's chest to support her as she pulled her ankle up to slip off her heels.

"I could say the same thing about you," Kale said as he watched her intently.

She leaned back up, holding her heels in one hand, and narrowed her eyes at him. "Well, go get the fucking car. I'm not walking across the parking lot barefoot, and my feet are killing me."

Kale tried not to smile, knowing good and well that it would tick her off, but it was a lost cause. It seemed as if this woman had a hard time telling him no.

FIVE

Light from the window poured into Ronnie's bedroom and although it wasn't a particularly sunny day, the brightness coated the space in a dim white glow that irritatingly caused Ronnie's eyes to flutter open.

She lay in her bed and stared at the ceiling, begging her mind to shut off and for a few more clouds to form in the sky so she could catch another hour or so of sleep. Once it was apparent that particular option was out of the question, Ronnie reached over to her nightstand and grabbed her phone. It was only nine in the morning and she hated to get out of bed until at least ten on Sundays, but it seemed like today she would be making an exception.

She rolled out of bed and her thighs felt tight, instantly reminding her about her continuous dancing the night before. Her mind wandered to the way Kale's large hands spread across her stomach as they slowly crept lower, stretching from hip to hip until the tips of his fingers touched right above the spot that was aching to be touched again. Then she thought about his damn mouth. It was sinful how good it was.

His lips were perfect; his top lip had a sharp cupid's bow and the bottom was just full enough for a man. And fuck, he knew how to use them. The way he ran them across her body and the way they felt against her own lips was enough to make the ache between her legs throb with the memory.

Damn it, that man was frustrating—in more ways than one. He knew just how to push her too, and for only knowing him a few days that was saying a lot. Ronnie didn't get her feathers ruffled too often; it took a strong personality to do that and Kale sure had it down pat.

The way he looked at her was something completely new to her. She was used to having men look at her as if they were selecting their choice of meat, but Kale didn't. He still looked at her like he was starving, but he didn't make her feel like a walking visual sex toy. It was like he cherished her with his eyes, like he was looking at her to ingrain her in his memory. It was hot, and it was terrifying.

Thank God, he hadn't asked to come inside when he dropped her off last night. She was walking a thin line with him and pair that with the Patrón that was running through her veins and she wasn't sure she would have woken up alone this morning—with clothing on for that matter—if he had asked.

She padded to her bathroom, stopping every few steps to stretch out her legs. The shower was calling to her like a siren and her tight muscles flexed under her skin in anticipation of the beating water.

By the time she stepped into the shower, her bathroom had turned into a scalding sauna, the water hot enough to boil her blood. She rested her forehead against the moist tile and let the hot water pulse against her. She used this time to burrow the thought of Kale away. The water pounded on her back and trickled down her body and fuck, it felt so good, she just may stay there all day.

After all the hot water was gone, Ronnie got out only sliding right back into pajamas. She put her favorite pair of baggy, gray, holey sweatpants on and slipped into a T-shirt that had exceeded its life expectancy, but she couldn't bear to throw out. Yes, it was one of Brandon's old shirts, but it was big and comfy and soft. It was so worn down that the cotton was basically see-through it was so thin.

As she was brushing out her damp hair, her phone lit up with an incoming call.

"Hello?" she asked, sitting down on the edge of her bed.

"Finally you answer your phone. What in the world have you been doing? I've been calling you for, like, the last hour."

"I was taking a shower."

"For an hour?"

"Pretty much. What do ya need, Jordan?"

"Nothing. I just wanted to make sure you got home okay," Jordan said.

"Yeah, no thanks to Cameron," Ronnie huffed. She didn't really give a shit that Jordan and Cameron left without her. It wasn't the first time she had to get her own way home from a bar, but it pissed her off a little that Cameron got that fucked-up to begin with. Ronnie was all for having a good time, but there's a line that needs to be drawn at some point, and he had passed it and was coming around for lap two.

"I'm sorry about that. He was being an idiot, running his mouth to one of the guys that tried to dance with us."

"That's why they threatened to call the cops?"

"Yeah, I was waiting for you by the doors of the club, and you know that big guy that was wearing the green shirt? Well, he walked out and made another pass at me while Cameron was waiting in the cab. Cameron saw him and got out with guns blazing."

"Well, damn, now I'm pissed I missed that," Ronnie said, laughing, her mood shifting when she learned that the reason they left in a hurry was because Cameron was defending his woman.

Jordan laughed with her. "Yeah, it was pretty hot seeing my man go all protective and territorial, but he still didn't get any drunken sex."

"Look at you standing your ground. I'm so proud."

"Yes, and it wasn't an easy task." She laughed. "Okay, so what I want to know is what the hell tattoo guy was doing at the club . . . dancing with you?" Jordan asked, changing the subject.

Ronnie rolled her eyes and fell back onto her bed. "He was stalking me. He knew I was going to be there," she said flatly.

"Well, it didn't look like you minded all that much."

"Fuck you, Jordan."

Jordan rolled with a high-pitched laugh. "Okay, so now I really know that you didn't mind. So what, he just comes to the club and gets grabby with you and you let him? That doesn't sound like you, Ronnie, unless—"

"Unless nothing," Ronnie interrupted.

"—unless you have already messed around with him. You have, haven't you? In the design room? I knew you were acting weird!"

"It was a mistake, and it didn't get too far anyway," Ronnie said, forcing herself not to let her mind go back there again.

"Why? He is gorgeous, Ronnie. I know he isn't the typical *thug* you seem to go for. So what if he's not tatted up from head to toe and doesn't look like he belongs in an orange jumpsuit? He looks like a really nice guy: you could use one for a change." Her voice was accusatory and dripping with repulsion. Jordan and Ronnie didn't exactly see eye-to-eye when it came to their taste in men.

"I never said he wasn't a nice guy. But you're right, he's a pretty boy, completely not my type, and he's a soldier. I'm not traveling down that road again."

"Not all soldiers are lying, cheating assholes like Brandon," Jordan said, not even attempting to hide the venom in her voice for how she felt about Brandon.

"No shit, Jordan, but soldiers are also always leaving. It doesn't fucking matter anyway." Ronnie pushed the words out between her teeth, hoping Jordan would know not to push the subject anymore.

"Whatever you say," Jordan said, annoyed. "Well, I'm gonna get off here. Cameron is taking me out so I need to go get ready. See you tomorrow morning?"

"Yep, see you tomorrow."

"All right. Happy Valentine's Day," she said in a singsong voice.

"Fucking kill me," Ronnie replied, rolling her eyes and shaking her head.

Jordan just laughed before she hung up the phone.

Ronnie sat up on her bed and looked around her room. She had a mound of laundry to do and it probably wouldn't hurt to run the vacuum, but fuck it. Her kitchen was clean, as always, and thanks to the lack of male reproductive organs using her bathrooms these days, those were clean as well. She could put off laundry for another day or so. Yep, she wasn't doing shit today.

This was the one day that Ronnie became a complete and utter shut-in. She shut out the colorful outside world that was gushing with love and romance and cupid's arrows, and she planted herself firmly in front of the TV wrapped up in her snuggie.

Ronnie was not one of those women who hated Valentine's Day because it was so depressing and only reminded her that she was alone and that she had no one to take her out or buy her gifts or bring her flowers. No, she had never given a shit about any of that stuff to begin with. She never particularly cared about Valentine's Day. It was never something she insisted on partaking in. But now she loathed it. It was a bunch of bullshit. It's an excuse for women to whine and dote and bat their eyelashes for glittery gifts in the hopeful forms of diamonds. It's an excuse for men to have an opening for sex, and all of its overkill, forced, mushy romance is sickening. What, just because it's a certain day that means the masks come off and men are suddenly thoughtful and romantic? Bullshit. If they weren't the other 364 days of the year then hate to break it to ya, they weren't sincere and they probably hated it just as much as Ronnie did. Most of the time, women were handed a proverbial gift in the form of romance that was wrapped up in a pink scented bow, tied with tape that was gonna sting like a motherfucker when you ripped it off, and then they were all upset and disappointed when it wasn't what they expected. It was actually quite funny, and it was also something Ronnie wanted nothing to do with.

It was lunchtime and Ronnie had ordered a couple pizzas. She popped in *A Nightmare on Elm Street* and grabbed a beer from the fridge. No judging, it was noon.

Ronnie propped her feet up on the leather ottoman in front of her couch, exposing her freshly painted wine red toenails and ripped open a bag of Reese's minis. That's another thing she hated about Valentine's Day: the fucking candy supply disappears at an alarming rate. She'd had to stop at two gas stations and finally Kinney Drugstore the other day to find one single bag. Fucking love vultures.

She was just getting into the movie, filling her mouth with peanut butter–filled chocolate—now that was one thing that she liked with her chocolate—and drinking her second beer when the doorbell rang. She hopped up from the couch and went to the kitchen for her purse.

"It's about time," she said as she was digging through her bag for her wallet. "You were cutting it pretty close, a few more minutes and it would've been free! It'd better be hot!" she hollered, walking to the front door.

She opened the door prepared to give the pizza guy a

mouthful when her jaw dropped and her heart slammed so hard against her ribs it knocked the air out of her lungs. What the fuck was he doing here?

Leaning against her doorframe looking like he stepped out of an American Eagle ad was Kale. He was wearing enough damn layers to stay warm in a fucking snowstorm, but it looked surprisingly good. He had a red long sleeve shirt under a gray fleece zip-up hoodie and topped off with a navy blazer. It was casual meets . . . shit she didn't even know: sexy, maybe? Yeah, that pretty much summed it up. And that fucking lopsided grin was in place, dimple and all protruding on his scruffy face.

"It'll be hot, I promise," he said, taking a step into her house.

"Kale."

"Happy Valentine's Day, Ronnie." He smiled at her and she wanted to curse the greater power in the world that thought it would be comical for her mind to want to slam the door in this soldier's face yet with the single twitch of his perfectly crafted lips her hormones wanted to slam her body into his instead.

"I don't do Valentine's Day, I told you," she spat at him, still pissed that with every inch he moved closer to her, her body betrayed her even more.

"Yeah, I remember," he said flatly, like he didn't care or like it didn't matter. "I still don't get it, though." This time when he talked his jaw flexed with the tension of suppressing a grin.

"You don't need to get it."

"Humor me," he said, finally allowing his lips to extend

into that panty-dropping smile, the one that was equal parts playful and determination. It made her instantly think of the way he smiled when he undressed her . . .

She blinked hard and snapped back to the present. "Valentine's Day is for hopeless romantics and pathetic saps. It's for people wanting all the proverbial hearts and flowers of love. It's fake and it's bullshit."

"I disagree."

She crossed her arms over her chest. "Somehow that doesn't surprise me."

"It's a day that is dedicated to that feeling you get when you are around that special someone," he said, taking an infinitesimal step toward her. "It's a day you can put all the other things aside and just feel. It doesn't have to be about flowers or jewelry or love. It can just be about two people."

"And you think that there needs to be a specific day for that? See, it's an excuse."

Kale huffed out a low sensual laugh that made Ronnie's insides shutter. "No, I don't think there needs to be a specific day to be with someone."

Ronnie sighed and shook her head slightly, all the while standing in front of the door, blocking Kale from coming all the way inside. "What the hell do you want, Kale?" She was irritated and more than annoyed.

"You." That was all he said before he closed the small gap of space between them, slid his hand around her neck and gently pulled her into his arms.

"Kale," Ronnie started as his lips immediately found their way to her neck.

"Yeah?" he breathed against her skin. The warmth from his breath traveled all the way down her neck and made itself nice and cozy in the spot right between her thighs.

Ronnie pulled back from him a little, her muscles protesting—tightening as her body involuntarily hesitated. He tilted his head to the side to look at her, his blue eyes going dangerously dark. They were eyes that had the potential of blinding her in their stormy desires, yet it was ironically beguiling—which made it even more wrong.

"We can't—"

"Ronnie, stop thinking. Just feel." He walked forward with her still wrapped tightly in his arms. He kicked the door shut with his foot and pulled the hem of Ronnie's T-shirt up. Her arms involuntarily rose and he pulled her shirt off over her head before she even realized he was doing it.

"Damn, you're beautiful," he said, his eyes roaming over her bare breasts. Ronnie had forgotten she wasn't even wearing a bra.

He pulled a hand from the small of her back and raised it to her breast, softly tracing her already taut nipple with his thumb. She resisted the need to drop her head back and arch her breasts into his hands. She wasn't going to go there with him, she couldn't.

But then his hand left her breast and wrapped around the back of her neck again and she instantly missed the feel of his large hand palming her flesh. Kale tilted her neck back and leaned his head down, pressing his forehead to hers.

"I told you to stop thinking," he said, and with his mouth so fucking close to hers, it made it easy for her mind to finally stop thinking because it suddenly became clouded with the need to taste him. "I can tell you want this just as badly as I do. I haven't been able to get you out of my head since I had you on that couch."

And that was all it took for her to raise up on her tiptoes and kiss him. Her lips connected with his hard and esurient. A moan vibrated against her lips from Kale's as he pulled her body in closer to him.

Ronnie's hands were already on the move. She slipped them up inside his hoodie and pushed it, along with the blazer, down his shoulders. He removed his hands from her body only long enough to let them drop to the floor.

What was it about this man that had her throwing caution to the wind and letting herself be swept away in the gust? It was beyond her, and at this particular moment, she didn't care.

Her lips moved fast against his. It was as if she finally unlocked the chastity belt she had fastened around her mind. She couldn't deny her body what it wanted any longer. She hadn't had no-strings-attached sex since, well, ever, and the only pleasure she had had recently came from inside her bedside drawer. Just the thought of him inside her had her dripping with need.

"Damn, sweetheart," Kale sighed against her lips as she slowly ran her tongue across his. He was walking her farther into the house and it dawned on her that he didn't know where he was going, but she suddenly found it extremely difficult to remove her mouth from his. She had opened up Pandora's box.

The doorbell rang, apparently her pizza was here—and it was late.

Kale's eyes lifted toward the door.

"Bedroom," she finally said, instantly bringing his attention back to her as they stumbled backward into the living room. She nodded her head toward the hallway.

"Yes, ma'am." Kale's voice was husky and his face was contorted into a wry grin, his eyes beaming with imperative hunger and a little bit of victory.

His mouth twisted up even more and he grabbed her under her ass, tossing her over his shoulder.

Ronnie released a shocked squeal and she wanted to rip her own fucking vocal cords out when she heard the annoying sound escape from her throat. Kale laughed, only making it worse.

"What the fuck, Emerson!"

"You like it," he accused, with what she could only imagine was a sly smile on his face. He smacked her ass that was perched on top of his shoulder, making her jerk. And damn it, she liked it.

As soon as Kale was in her bedroom he dropped her onto her bed, causing her body to bounce on the mattress. "Don't be gentle by any means," she hissed.

"Don't worry, sweetheart. I don't plan to be."

She swallowed hard, her mind and her body playing a close game of tug-of-war with her conscience, but with Kale saying words like that, her body started to take the lead.

Ronnie propped up on her elbows and attempted to narrow her eyes at Kale but it was useless. He was already pulling his shirt off, and her eyes lost their previous intentions: they were now completely focused on his bare chest. He stepped out of his jeans and Ronnie sucked in a breath at the sight of his erection pressing against his boxer briefs. She inched back on the bed and she couldn't help the smile that took over the majority of her cheeks.

"Like what you see?" Kale let his smile tease the words. Um, hell yes, she did. His thighs were thick, his waist was narrow, and his chest was broad. He was definitely beautiful.

Ronnie didn't say anything, though. Admitting to him that she liked what she saw was almost as bad as admitting to him that she had wanted him from the first night she met him. And there was no way in hell that was going to fucking happen.

Kale just laughed, it was low and sexy, almost like it was intentional. He bent over, sliding his boxers down, and in one graceful movement he slid between her legs.

"Hips up," he said, grabbing ahold of the waistband of her sweats along with the unfortunate cotton panties she had put on today—it wasn't like she had anticipated getting naked with anyone, for crying out loud.

She did as he asked and he easily slipped them off her. She was sprawled out on the bed, completely naked, and this irritatingly sexy man was kneeling in between her legs. Her blood started flowing hot in her veins, swirling through her body, the heat gathering low in her stomach.

She watched as he reached down, grabbed his impressive length in his hand and rolled a condom down his thick shaft. He leaned down between her, his body sinking onto hers. The playfulness in his eyes was now ringed with an intensity that was raw and sexy and powerful and she could see the take-charge Sergeant First Class in him that she knew he was.

His head dipped down to her shoulder, kissing and sucking her sensitive skin. He smelled intoxicating, a light, woodsy cologne, and it made her light-headed in a way that had her wanting to be wrapped in his scent. She leaned her nose against his neck and breathed him in, grazing her teeth along his skin as she did.

Instantaneously she felt the head of his erection flex against her entrance. She raised her hips, begging for the invasion but he remained still, unmoving above her.

She groaned in aggravation: she needed him now. She didn't think she could wait another minute. "Kale."

"So eager all of a sudden?" He lifted his head up and looked at her, an impish gleam shining through his eyes.

He lowered his hand between their bodies and found the ache between her legs with his finger. He easily slipped it inside her, her silky arousal encasing him in wet warmth.

"Mmm," he moaned, the low hum tickling her flushed skin as he pressed his lips to the dip at her throat.

"Kale," she pleaded, her body squirming uncontrollably beneath him.

He didn't respond. It was like his name rolling out of her mouth was the signal he was waiting on. He withdrew his finger from her and slammed into her in one quick thrust, producing a sharp audible sigh from Ronnie. Yes, this is what she fucking wanted. Her insides wrapped tightly around his thickness and he slowly swiveled his hips while keeping himself pressed deep inside her as she stretched to accommodate him. As she moved her hips with him, he increased his speed, sinking into her hard and fast then pulling back only to repeat the delicious movement over and over and over.

His mouth found its way back to hers. It was demanding and consuming and anything but gentle. His tongue pushed its way inside her, deepening the kiss, claiming her—and Ronnie willingly reciprocated.

Her hands wound underneath his arms and she pressed her fingers to his back. Just as her fingers started to curl into his skin, he sucked in a quick breath and the muscles of his back tensed—but his hips never stopped moving.

"Shit, I'm so sorry," Ronnie said, jerking her hands from the freshly inked skin of his back.

Kale pulled his hips back agonizingly slowly, teasing her as the feel of him gradually leaving her left waves of silky pleasure in its place. Just as the very tip of him rested against her, he thrashed back into her, hitting that spot within her depths, causing all her other senses to give out. She threw her head back as she cried out.

Kale's tongue licked a trail up her throat as he went back to relentlessly pushing her closer and closer. "I don't have a problem with pain, baby. Touch me wherever your little heart desires," he whispered as his mouth reached her ear.

Holy fucking . . . he was driving her body insane. A pressure was building and she latched onto his shoulders, digging her nails into his skin.

"Yeah, baby, let go. I want to feel you come around me." He rolled his hips and then slammed back into her.

Her hips lifted to meet his as a rippled paroxysm of fire scorched to life between her thighs, bubbling over in waves.

Kale collapsed on top of her. His breathing was quick and heavy, matching her own breaths, and his chest and stomach bathed her in a thin layer of sweet moisture. After a few heartbeats, he rolled off her and pulled her to him. Her head lay in the crook of his neck and her legs were flung loosely in between his, their bodies tangling together. A part of her wanted to object, to tell him to back the fuck off, but her eyes were heavy and her body was spent. Her mind was in complete euphoria, plus the feel of his fingers gently raking through her hair made her scalp tingle and it made her eyes so tired it felt as if they were weighed down. Her body was riding on a hundred different sensations, and she didn't have the energy to protest or ponder the repercussions of them. So she just took a breath, and allowed her vision to slowly fade behind her tired lids.

Kale was jostled awake by a shove to his arm. He didn't have to open his eyes to know that a beautiful yet pissed-off Ronnie would be staring at him.

"Get up." She jabbed her palm into his biceps again and Kale just smiled. He reluctantly opened his eyes and stretched out his arms that were still wrapped around Ronnie as she tried to wiggle her way out of his hold.

"Hey."

"Think you could get off me?" she asked, trying once again to shift her body out from under him.

He laughed, pressing his hands onto the small of her back and holding her in a hug. He dipped his head down and kissed her once on her earlobe, quickly grazing it with his teeth before he let her go and rolled onto his back.

The dim light flowing in through the window was carrying with it the thick warmth of evening. Shit, they must have been asleep for a couple of hours.

"Okay," Ronnie said, sitting up, pulling the white sheet around her so it was covering her bare breasts. "We can't do this anymore. You've had your fun. I've had my fill. Now we can both go on our separate ways."

"You've had your fill?" he said, cocking his head to the side to look at her. Her face was impassive.

She rolled her eyes. "Yes, my curiosity is satisfied."

"You were curious about me?" He looked knowingly at her, and as he watched Ronnie's face turn from creamy to rosy, a pixilated smirk pulled across his cheeks.

"*Were* being the operative word—as in no longer. Look, this was fun. It was good—" Kale stalled her words as he arched his thick eyebrows at her, unconvinced by her choice of adjective. "Okay it was pretty fucking mind-blowing," she declared.

His eyes relaxed and his mouth slacked back into its original postcoital smile.

"But . . . that was it. We can't do this again."

He leaned up on his elbow. "And what is your reasoning for that, because there are more than a few reasons for why I think we should *definitely* do this again."

"I told you last night, I don't date."

"Who said we were dating?"

"No one said we were dating, but I'm also not a tramp who sleeps with different guys every night."

A possessive shrill slithered through Kale's nerve endings,

causing him to tense. “You won’t be sleeping with different guys. You’ll be sleeping with me.”

“No. I—”

“Ronnie, I get it. You don’t do the whole girlie thing. Lucky for you, I don’t do the whole relationship thing.”

“A guy not wanting to commit to one girl, shocker.”

She was throwing her ex issues in his face and he wasn’t going to let that happen. “That has absolutely nothing to do with it. I’m a firm believer in commitment, and I know what it entails and I know how hard it can be. I also know that adding the military to that equation makes it even more difficult. I don’t choose not to be in a relationship because I don’t want to be with one woman, I choose not to be in a relationship because when I decide to commit, I want to put that woman before everything else, just like it should be, and right now I can’t do that. Right now, I’m not ready to do that. So, committing to one woman isn’t the issue.” He reached under the covers and pulled Ronnie’s body down so that she was once again lying next to him. He ran his index finger up and down her stomach, igniting a patch of goose bumps on her naked skin.

“What’re you doing?” Her voice cracked a little as she tried to get the words out in a volume that was slightly louder than a whisper.

“Trying to remind you how I can make you feel. I want you to think about what you would be missing out on.”

Her eyes were dark and her breathing was forced, but her body was lax. She was soft under his hands; she was like warm, melting butter.

"I know how you make me feel," she said, blinking hard, scooting away from him.

"I'm only here for five more days, Ronnie. Don't ask me why, but I like being around your bad attitude and your smart mouth. You're entertaining."

"Oh, so glad I've provided you with a source of entertainment."

Kale sighed and shook his head. This damn woman was exhausting, but he already knew it was worth it. "I'd like to spend my last few days in the States with you. No fluffy stuff." His smile returned in full swing when she wrinkled her forehead in a question, so he elaborated, "I promise not to bring you flowers or take you to fancy restaurants or buy you gifts, and I promise I won't let you fall in love with me." He winked.

"Ha, like that would be a problem." She rolled her eyes and gave him a dastardly laugh. She paused for a minute, seeming to be weighing her options. Her naked breasts caused the sheet to rise and fall above them as she breathed and he could see her pulse pounding through the thin skin at her neck—and it was speeding up.

Her eyes shifted pensively toward the ceiling, and they stayed there long enough to make Kale restless. When she lowered them back to him, the chocolate color seemed to melt around the rim, turning to honey. "Okay, soldier, here's the deal. We can do this again only under the circumstances that we both understand that it's JUST SEX. No strings, no commitment, no dating. Just sex."

"It's what I do best, sweetheart." He tilted his lips into a lopsided grin, which generated one of his now expected responses, an eye roll from Ronnie.

"So do we agree then?" Ronnie asked. She seemed unsure in her own part in the agreement, like she was still teetering on the idea.

"Yes. Ronnie, I enjoy being around you, and I definitely enjoy being inside you." She pursed her lips together and cocked her head to the side, and it made Kale want to bite those full pouty lips of hers. "A strictly sex relationship is just what I need right now."

"Okay."

"Okay?"

"Yes, okay. Now, since your horrible timing of seduction interrupted my mealtime, I'd like to eat." Ronnie stood up, Kale's eyes getting a first glimpse of her glorious body in a vertical position. He could only think of one thing that would make her even sexier at that very moment, and it was an image of cherry red heels.

"You're mind-fucking me again," she admonished, pulling a tight Black Crowes concert T-shirt on over her head.

"How would you know what I'm thinking?"

Ronnie just laughed as she picked up her sweatpants from the floor and pulled them on.

Kale sauntered out of the bed and made his way to the foot of the bed where his clothes lay discarded on the floor. He watched as Ronnie gazed at him from the corner of her eyes.

"Now who is mind-fucking who?" he said, mocking her.

Ronnie tried to cover up her quickly blushing cheeks with an eye roll but she wasn't fooling anyone.

Kale smiled warmly and shook his head. "Come on, let's go grab some food."

"First of all, no dinner dates, remember? Second of all, my ass doesn't leave the house on Valentine's Day, especially to go out to eat. If I have to look at one couple staring lovingly into each other's eyes, I'm likely to fucking lose it."

Kale shook his head. "Okay, well, we both need to eat at some point."

"I do have a kitchen you know. It comes equipped with things like a refrigerator, a stove, even an oven."

Hum, sarcastic Ronnie was just a sexy as impudent Ronnie.

"Okay, sweetheart. Care to feed me?" he asked, walking to the bedroom door, looking back for Ronnie to follow.

She sighed. "Your ass is doing the dishes."

SIX

Kale hadn't had a meal like that for an extremely long and overdue amount of time. He had sat at the bar and watched Ronnie gracefully prance around the kitchen, preparing dinner and cooking with ease. He listened to her talk about her love for art and about her job, which of course went hand in hand. She talked about her friends, which he learned were all men except for the small blonde he'd met yesterday, and for some reason, that little fact didn't sit too well with him.

The easy way she held a conversation with him while she was cooking was new. It was refreshing to see her less tense—her guard slightly down. He was still sailing through choppy waters, but he could see the calm up ahead, and he was getting closer to reaching it.

"Where in the world did you learn to cook like that?" Kale asked, loading their dishes into the dishwasher.

It was Ronnie's turn to sit at the bar, and she was drinking a beer while watching him. "I've been cooking since I was old enough to reach the dial on the oven with a step stool.

Thanks to my alcoholic mother, who was never sober enough to stand, I've had lots of practice. You should try my mac and cheese." She fiddled with her hands, which were resting on top of the bar. Her eyes were fixed downward, focusing on her hands like she was lost in her own head.

Kale didn't know what it was like to have a mother, but he'd had a damn good grandmother. She had taken such good care of him and enjoyed doing it that he'd never had to want for anything, especially a meal. He had no idea what it was like to grow up without someone to take care of you in the way family does. It may have just been him and his grandmother, but she had been enough.

"What about your dad?" The second the words trickled out of his mouth he could feel acid rolling off her in thick deadly sheets and he immediately regretted asking.

"Don't fucking know, don't fucking care."

Kale turned around. He knew he had struck a nerve, and he cursed to himself when he saw the way Ronnie's shoulders seemed to slump over, her brown eyes sad. "Sorry. I didn't mean to—"

"No," Ronnie interrupted before he could finish his apology. "There's nothing to be sorry for, so don't. I never knew the man. Hell, I'm not even sure if my mom even knew who my father was."

"Do you ever see her?"

Ronnie shook her head and took a long pull from her beer. "I haven't seen nor have I talked to her since I left that fucking place, six years ago. I don't intend to either."

Damn. He was beginning to see that this woman had a

lot more buried under the surface than her tough, tattooed skin allowed to show through.

"So where to next?" Kale wanted to change the subject, stir her thoughts in a different direction than painful ones that filled the current space of her mind. More than that, he wanted to try to sneak back into the tight, placid bubble of ease that Ronnie was in only moments ago.

She lifted her eyes to him and blinked. "What?"

Kale dried his hands on the dishtowel and took the few steps to the bar, leaning his elbows down on the cool gray granite.

"You mentioned that you were planning on selling your house and moving. Where to?"

She sighed. "Hell, anywhere but here. I don't want to be in the same town with my ex for any longer than I have to. Take my advice, never put your name on a mortgage with someone. I'm not even married to Brandon and I feel like we're going through a damn divorce. Once his sorry ass gets back here we can officially put the house up for sale and hopefully I'll be long gone before he gets home for good."

Okay, an indirect answer, and it definitely didn't stir her thoughts to a more pleasant direction. Plan B.

"So, I brought you something."

"What do you mean you brought me something?" She looked genuinely pissed. He couldn't catch a damn break.

Kale held up his hands as if surrendering to the lashing that he was all too certain Ronnie was perfectly capable of dealing out.

"Damn it, soldier. I don't want any gifts."

"It's not a gift." He walked out of the kitchen and into the entryway where his blazer lay disheveled on the floor. He pulled out a small slender rectangle from the inside pocket and carried it back into the kitchen, hiding it in his hands behind his back.

Kale stood next to Ronnie and attempted like hell not to burst out in a laugh at the way she was sending him a death look with her mouth pursed together and her arms crossed over her chest. He pulled his hands around front, holding his nongift out for her to see.

He wanted to sigh in relief when Ronnie smiled wide, unable to hide her amusement from him even if she wanted to. "Are you fucking serious right now?" She laughed.

"Serious as a heart attack. Figured I might as well see what all the hype is about this sparkling vampire stuff."

"You want to watch *Twilight*?" She wasn't buying his attempt at honesty, and she was hitting the nail on the head.

"No," he admitted. "But I remember you saying you liked it, and I thought I could win you over with this if you didn't let me through the front door. But obviously it was unnecessary." He winked at her and watched as she hopped off her barstool and stood agonizingly close to him. Her body just being in the same sliver of space as his had his body rising.

Ronnie took the movie from him. "Smart thinking there, soldier."

He shoved his hands in his pockets and smiled. "Shit, I'm just thankful you didn't say you were a secret fan of *The Notebook*. I've always pitied my buddies who got suckered into that one."

Ronnie turned her head around to look at him. A small smile tugged at her mouth as she bit the corner of her bottom lip. How could one small little movement cause such a strong reaction from him? The way her eyes looked up from her lashes, the way her long hair fell over her shoulder as she looked at him, the way her teeth pulled on her lip, it all circulated a throb—one that sent all his blood to his groin.

"Oh please, tell me you're not."

She laughed. "Sorry, no can do."

Kale followed her to the living room, sat down on the overstuffed couch, and stretched his arms out. He watched as Ronnie bent over to put the DVD in. Her overly large sweats that swallowed her were hung low on her hips and her shirt was so tight that it pulled up slightly as she leaned down. He noticed another tattoo peeking out from the top of her pants just below the bottom of the dream-catcher tattoo and he made a mental note to explore every inch of her body so he could find every last trace of art on her skin.

Kale had never been a huge fan of tattoos on women. The occasional so-called tramp stamp or ankle tattoo was okay. He was even used to seeing small tattoos on the inside of women's wrists, but for the most part, he preferred their skin to be smooth and clear and supple. But Ronnie on the other hand, she was breaking all of his "typical type" ideals. He found himself wanting to study her body, to trace his finger over every line of every tattoo that covered her. From the one on her left shoulder that traveled all the way down her arm, to the large one covering the span of her back, to the one on her right side that continued down her hip and onto her thigh, and to the one placed dangerously low right above her ass. They were beautiful and they were even more beautiful on her body.

"Hello?" Ronnie said, staring at him from across the room next to the TV.

"Sorry. What?" Kale blinked to pull the image of Ronnie's naked body from his ruttish mind so he could focus on Ronnie who was in front of him.

"I asked if you wanted another beer. Fuck, I don't offer to serve people often and you've had sex and dinner already: you're pushing your luck."

"Well, in that case, I'd better take you up on your offer while it's still in good standing."

When Ronnie came back in the room, she handed him a beer and then sat down at the other end of the couch, as far away from Kale as she possibly could be without sitting on the floor.

The movie was actually pretty good, although Kale would never admit it. Apparently he had purchased the third movie in the series when he didn't even realize there was more than one, so Ronnie had to spend a good portion of the beginning of the movie getting him up to speed.

Somewhere in the middle, Ronnie curled her legs up to the side of her as she was leaning into the armrest. Her delicate feet were in arm's reach of Kale and he was itching to touch her. He bit the bullet and grabbed Ronnie's ankle, pulling her closer to him. Her head whipped around to look at him, but she didn't say anything, which shocked the hell out of him. He was fully expecting an ass chewing.

"I can't be this close to you and not touch you," he said. He wasn't going to apologize, he wanted her and he was going to get her while he could, any part of her that he could. He pulled her legs onto his lap and she silently and carefully watched him as he picked up her foot and started rubbing her instep.

"Mmm, keep doing that and you can touch me all you want," she said with a moan as she shut her eyes and leaned the side of her head against the back of the couch.

Kale slowly rubbed the soles of her feet, finding all the spots that made her sigh, and the spots that made her giggle. He worked one and then the other, watching as her breaths got short and even the more and more relaxed she got.

"This isn't some ploy to get me back in the bedroom is it?" Her eyes were still shut and her voice was soft and raspy.

"That wasn't my intention but I'd be happy to oblige," Kale said, working his way slowly up her calf.

"I don't think I'll be able to move my body. This feels so good." Her words slowly slurred together as sleep was stretching out to her.

Making her succumb to sleep by the touch of his fingers gave Kale a pleasure that ran hot in his bones. He continued to massage her for just a few more minutes, and then he gently lowered her feet to the floor and slipped a hand around her waist.

Her eyes popped open when he started pulling her to him.

"Come here," he said, tucking her under his arm. Her body was suddenly rigid like she wasn't quite sure of the idea.

"Let me hold you." He buried his nose in her hair and

took a deep breath in. The smell of vanilla and coconut with a little bit of citrus filled his lungs.

For a long moment Ronnie didn't say anything. She was frozen solid, her eyes never moving from his, but gradually her body relaxed and she allowed Kale to pull her the rest of the way to him. The second her body collided with his, she wedged herself in close to his side and nuzzled his chest. She fit next to him perfectly, and he held her to him like that until he heard soft feminine snores coming from her.

Kale debated whether or not to lean back and spend the night with this woman wrapped in his arms. Having a soft, warm body next to him while he slept was something he always loved, even if he always wanted that body to leave first thing in the morning. But he knew Ronnie wouldn't want that. Even if it was just a physical need, something his body craved, it wouldn't be that way for her. Everything seemed to register differently for women, hell, every man knew that. But where some women would love to spend the night curled up next to a man, even when they knew it was nothing more than two bodies touching, he knew Ronnie wouldn't see it that way. Kale was pretty sure cuddling was on the "can't do" list for their little arrangement.

Kale lifted her easily in his arms, pressing her against his chest as he carried her to her bedroom. She didn't stir until he laid her down in the bed.

He ran his knuckles down the side of her cheek. "Good night."

"Good night," Ronnie said; her voice was raspy from being asleep and it was sexy. She smiled at him, a real one, one that he hadn't seen since last night when she appraised the tattoo on his back. He liked it. It worked well for her. Kale smiled back and turned to walk out of the bedroom door.

"Happy Valentine's Day," he whispered as he walked out the door and he was almost positive he heard her say it back.

SEVEN

Two more to go.

Ronnie's feet pounded one after the other. She felt the pleasing pull in her thighs, that subtle hurts-so-good kind of burn, and she pushed the button on the treadmill increasing the incline. She had to hit four miles today. She'd finished off a six-pack of beer yesterday and damn near destroyed the entire bag of Reese's; four miles was the bare minimum.

Running was Ronnie's way of kicking her own ass. It was also a way to get out of her head. She knew most people ran to think, to hear nothing but the voice in their head, but the last fucking thing Ronnie wanted to hear was her own voice bitching inside her head. No, running was Ronnie's escape, her solitude. When she ran she shut off, the only thing switched on was her legs. She would push herself until the muscles in her legs could no longer support her weight, or until her lungs screamed out in agony—whichever came first. The only noise she heard was from the sound of her feet pounding the pavement—or the belt of the treadmill in this case—and the sound of the instrumental piano playing on the Pandora station on her iPhone, lulling her mind into oblivion.

A heavy coating of sweat covered Ronnie's face and chest by the time she slowed the speed of the treadmill at four and a half miles. She much preferred to run outdoors, but the cold, winter New York weather could kiss her ass. No way in hell was she going outside longer than necessary.

She walked another half mile then stepped off and headed for the gym's classroom. Yoga was her second sanctuary of solitude and she taught a class at the gym on post every Monday at six thirty a.m. She wasn't a morning person. She actually hated waking up early, but the six thirty morning class had the smallest turnout and the most dedicated women. Some of them were soldiers, but the majority of them were Army wives. The other classes were later in the day and completely filled with chatty, gossip-thriving women who would rather stick their noses up at Ronnie and her cleavage-showing tank top and the full sleeve on her arm than do the class.

Contrary to her feelings about the majority of the female species, she actually liked the women in her a.m. class. Hell, she had the utmost respect for military spouses (even the ones who were complete bitches to her), knowing good and well the shit these women had to go through for their families. Don't get the wrong idea, she wasn't running off to FRG meetings and wine Wednesdays with these women, but she liked them nonetheless.

Ronnie passed the wandering eyes of the usual Monday morning crowd of soldiers that were doing part of their PT in the weight room before stopping short as she reached the free weights. A back with an all too familiar tattoo of sentimental poetry and ripped flesh was standing in front of her, arms stretched up, holding on to a chin-up bar.

She hoisted her hand on her hip and paused for the show. The muscles in his shoulders bulged and flexed as he pulled his body up and down, causing the muscles in his back to ripple underneath the beauty of the ink. Watching the wide span of his back move underneath the tattoo was mesmerizing. His body was sculpted like the gods themselves carved him by hand.

She audaciously studied him, committing each dip and curve and edge of him to her memory, tucking it away for her lonely nights.

After doing countless amounts of pull-ups, Kale released his hands and dropped to the ground. His body was dripping with sweat as he reached for his towel. When he turned around his eyes immediately found hers and he smiled her favorite one yet, a surprised, lopsided grin.

She stayed planted in place, her hand still on her hip, her eyes still appraising him as he took the few long strides to her.

"Hey," he said, wiping the perspiration from his face.

"Hey, yourself," she said, unable to look away from the hard body covered in sweat standing perilously close to her.

"What're you doing here? I didn't peg you as the early-riser type."

"Yeah, you pegged right. I'm not an early riser, but I teach a yoga class here every Monday at six thirty."

"Yoga, huh?"

"Yeah. You interested?"

"In watching you do yoga, absolutely."

Ronnie's infamous eye roll came swinging through full force. "No, in participating, jackass."

He chuckled. "Um, no. But I will, however, sit my happy 'jackass' down on this weight bench and gladly watch you participate," he said, bouncing his eyebrows up and down.

"Yeah, I'm sure you would."

Jordan took that moment to make her appearance. She jogged up to them and stopped next to Ronnie. "Hey, Ronnie." She looked at Kale, her face having a physical debate on whether to smile or frown at him. "He really is stalking you, isn't he?" she asked, completely serious.

It was Kale's turn to frown. "What?"

"Yes, he is," Ronnie laughed. "I'll see you later." She smiled at Kale and he pinned her with a look that made her already-flushed face turn another shade of pink.

"Seriously, what is he doing here?" Jordan asked as they walked into the classroom.

"What the fuck do you think he is doing? He's working out."

"Did you tell him you were going to be here? I'm starting to get creeper vibes from him, but I'm almost willing to overlook it because of how sexy he looks all hot and sweaty. And did you see the way he was looking at you? Damn, girl."

"Jordan. Stop running your mouth . . . please. No, I didn't tell him I was going to be here, he was probably here before I was—he's not a creeper—and, yes, I saw the way he looked at me."

Jordan turned her head over her shoulder to get a last look at Kale, who was now sitting on the bench curling dumbbells.

"I think I like him," Jordan said when her head was back in alignment with the front of her body.

"You just said you got creeper vibes. Make up your damn mind."

"Well, creeper or not, he's sexy."

Ronnie glanced over her shoulder to see Kale's stare burning into her. He didn't smile or wink or anything else playfully sexy like she expected him to do when she met his eyes. Instead, he just kept her gaze, locking her in with his stormy blue eyes that seemed to consume her. It was intense and hot and it made Ronnie feel powerful.

After the last few of her regulars arrived, Ronnie began the class. She was all too aware of Kale's eyes on her through the floor-length windows that made up the wall separating the gym from the classroom. It was hot knowing he was watching her, and it made her body go on high alert. It was intense and exhilarating. She did every pose like she was doing it for him; it wasn't something that she was doing intentionally, but it was like her body knew he was watching her and it zinged to life.

She transitioned from half moon to standing bow and held her pose. It was as if she could feel the heat traveling from the tip of her extended toe through the fingertips of her extended arm. It was the most erotic yoga class she had ever taught and Kale wasn't even in the room with her. Her body burned, not just from the workout, but also from the thick tension that linked them through a sheet of glass. Every now and again, she would catch his stare through the reflection of the mirror; the hunger in his eyes was unmistakable and it made for the sexiest and longest class of her life.

When the class was over and Ronnie was once again covered in a thin layer of sweat, she walked out of the classroom and nailed Kale with a knowing glance. He immediately followed her to the opposite end of the back wall to the locker rooms.

Kale walked behind Ronnie, knowing exactly what she was up to. Even though he wouldn't be able to partake in the events that he knew were about to unfold, he still couldn't help wanting to see just what she had up her sleeve.

Ronnie turned the corner at the end of the back wall and led him down a hallway. She pushed open a door and peeked her head in, then grabbed his hand pulled him inside. The door wasn't even completely shut before she pressed her body against him. The urgency in the way she touched him had him wishing he could rip the damp clothes from her body. But they couldn't. Not here. Not in a military building full of soldiers. Even though they were in the women's locker room, he was sure that if anyone walked in on them they would be only too eager to talk about the SFC who was taking a woman in the locker room.

Before he could even get a word out in a piss-poor attempt to protest, she had her full lips covering his. She dug both hands into the back of his neck and pulled him down to her so she could kiss him deeper. How this woman could make him forget every coherent thought that was streaming through his head was beyond him, but the taste of her sweet breath mixed with the salty dew on her body was intoxicating.

He doltishly slid his hands around her waist and cupped her ass, bringing her even tighter against him. He could feel his body rising in his shorts and having Ronnie's body rubbing against him wasn't helping.

"Fuck, Ronnie, I don't know how much more I can take, sweetheart."

"Take it all. I'm activating our just-sex policy."

Kale groaned as she slid her hand in between their bodies and rubbed it against his aching bulge. Damn it, he didn't want her to stop.

Ronnie's hair was conveniently tied back into a ponytail, her long waves hanging down her neck and brushing the top of her back. He twisted the hair in his hand and gently yanked back, pinning her head so her mouth was no longer on his. She let out a satisfied yelp and the fact that she liked the little tug made a vision of things he would like to do to her run through his mind. Oh, what he could do to this woman.

With her head tilted back trapped by his hand, he took that moment to trail his tongue up the center of her throat, deliciously tasting the sweet salty moisture that clung to her skin.

"I'm not going to take you here," he whispered against her flesh. He released her hair and her head dropped down so she was now looking him in the eyes.

"What?"

"We're not doing this here," he said, and even as the words left his mouth, he wished he didn't have to say them.

Ronnie was pissed, she was pouting and fuck, it was sexy, but against every man code there was about not questioning it when a beautiful bombshell pushes you in an empty locker room for sex, he just couldn't do it. Not only were the ramifications of an NCO having sex in a public government building reason enough to not go through with her little temptation; the very thought of someone coming in and seeing her like that made his blood boil. No, no one was going to see her but him; he wasn't going to chance it.

"I thought random spontaneous fucking was what guys dreamed of."

Kale couldn't help laughing. Yes, this was normally right up his alley.

Ronnie took a step back from him and sighed. "Now I'm all wound up."

"I'll take care of that tonight. Believe me, baby, I'm dying here too." He looked at her swollen lips and her full breasts and he damn near said fuck it, but he forced himself to stay strong.

"I can't see you tonight. I'm working late and then I'm finishing up a piece on Mic."

"Mic?" he asked with a hiccup of a territorial growl forming in the base of his throat.

"Yes, Mic. The fifty-year-old bald guy with a beer belly and a cigarette permanently hanging out of his mouth . . ."

Kale relaxed. Oh, yeah, Mic.

"Do you work tomorrow? I want you to go somewhere with me."

Ronnie raised her eyebrows. "Kale, I thought we discussed this. I don't want to go on any dates."

"It's not a date. I'm driving to my hometown to visit my grandmother. It's a four-hour drive each way and I just want you to keep me company on the road trip."

"Meeting family definitely doesn't fall into the just-sex part of our relationship. Sorry."

"I know, and you wouldn't be meeting her. You can even stay in the car. I just want to lay some flowers on her grave."

Ronnie wanted to slap herself in the face for being such a stupid bitch. This guy who had annoyingly wedged his way into her life was asking her to go with him to visit his grandmother's grave site and she was being completely insensitive. Did she want to go? Fuck no. The thought of being in a car for four hours sounded torturous, and spending time at a cemetery wasn't on her list of enjoyable activities. But there was a sadness in Kale's eyes that was hauntingly beautiful and she could tell that he didn't want to go alone. Damn it.

"Fuck . . . okay, I'll go with you, but I have a shop meeting at ten thirty tomorrow morning, so we can't leave until around noon."

Kale's dimple appeared. "Thank you." The words mirrored his smile as he scooped her back into his arms. His bare chest and tight arms held her so tightly that they squeezed all thoughts from her head, leaving only the need she had for him. She slipped her hands over the sharp angles of his hips and over the deep mountains of his stomach. She tilted her head up, ran her tongue over the stubble of his chin and tasted his salty skin. He groaned and she felt his erection spring back to life against her stomach. She couldn't help trying her luck one last time so she slid her hand down his shorts and grabbed his thick length in her hand.

"Baby . . ." Kale started to protest and he gently pulled her hand up out of his shorts.

As per her usual, Jordan took that moment to come bounding through the door, interrupting them once again. "Oh, um . . . sorry . . ."

Kale leaned down and whispered in Ronnie's ear, "Now I'm all wound up."

"Serves you right for denying me." She smirked.

"All right, sweetheart," he said, laughing. "I'll see you tomorrow."

After Kale walked out of the locker room, Jordan fixed her wide-eyed, arched eyebrows at Ronnie.

"Don't even," Ronnie spat.

"All right, all right."

"So what's up? You looked like you were on a mission when you stormed in here."

"Oh . . . yeah . . . well . . ."

"Spit it out, Jordan," Ronnie reprimanded, taking her annoyance for her sexual frustration out on Jordan.

"Mic called, he's been trying to get ahold of you."

"At seven forty-five in the morning? I didn't know Mic knew how to function this early in the morning. What did he want?"

"Well, um . . ."

Ronnie just narrowed her eyes at her friend; she seriously needed to get on with it already.

"Brandon has been calling the shop and now he has started calling Mic's cell phone." Her voice held an apology as if her words would slice open an old wound. They kind of did.

"When the fuck did Brandon start calling the shop? And why didn't anyone tell me?"

"A few days ago, but Mic took care of it. He didn't want you to get upset and he told that son of a bitch to leave you the hell alone. He had his calls blocked from the shop line, but now that he is trying to get ahold of you through his cell phone, Mic thought you should know."

"Fucking asshole. Okay, thanks, Jordy."

"You all right?" she asked softly, and Ronnie hated that Jordan was worried about her.

Ronnie planted an indifferent expression on her face and strutted toward the locker room door. "Yep, I'm good." And she was going to be, even if it fucking killed her.

"So you want to explain to me why you thought it was fucking smart to keep from me the little fact that Brandon was blowing up the shop phone?" Ronnie asked as she stormed into Mic's room. Everyone else was gone for the night so it was finally safe for Ronnie to unleash her wrath. She couldn't believe her best friend would hide the fact that her ex-fiancé was repeatedly calling. And what pissed her off even more was that she wanted to know what Brandon wanted. She didn't want to care, she didn't want to give a shit, but she did.

"You don't need to talk to his sorry ass, Angel. What could he possibly have to say to you that would fucking matter anyway?" Mic pulled the transfer paper of the last portion of his back piece out of the drawer in his filing cabinet next to the counter and slammed it shut.

"Well, the last time I checked I was still in control of my own decisions. I could've handled him."

"But I didn't want you to have to deal with him if you didn't have to. I took care of it. If you wanted to stay in touch with him then you shouldn't have changed your phone number." Mic stood up and stepped past Ronnie into the hall.

Ronnie stepped into the doorway. "What did he want, Mic? What did he say?" Her voice was soft and she could hear the sad, pathetic plea in her tone and she wanted to curse and scream and bawl her eyes out for letting Brandon get to her once again.

Mic stopped dead in his tracks and turned back to her until he was standing right in front of her. "I don't know, Angel. I didn't ask and he probably wouldn't have told me even if I had."

"He was your friend too, Mic."

"I renounced that title from him the second he fucked you over. He fucking destroyed you. I could never be friends with anyone who would hurt you."

"Because I let him destroy me. He was all I ever knew. He was all I ever had. Until him, I lived with a woman who was always so drunk she could never remember my name. I didn't have any girlfriends. They were either jealous bitches who treated me like a freak, or they succumbed to the trailer-trash druggies they were destined for. And the guys, they just wanted to fuck me. I was alone. Completely fucking alone."

She sighed and her voice lowered. "Then I met Brandon and he changed everything for me. He gave me hope for a life other than the shithole that was burying me alive. Then he gave it to me only to rip it out from under me when he fucked the first woman who would spread her legs for him." Ronnie sagged her body against the doorframe, letting it hold her weight as she focused on keeping the weak tears in the back of her eyes.

"Did you love him, Ronnie, or did you love the idea of him?"

She blinked hard and tried to pull air down her burning throat to fill her deflated lungs. She hadn't really ever thought about it like that. She did love him, right? She did, she knew she did. He was her family. He was her future. But at the same time, she never got shivers when he touched her, and she never melted into his arms. She never burned with an ache for him that would only be alleviated by his body buried inside her. She never craved him. Not like the way Kale made her feel. But that was just physical, it wasn't what really mattered, and at least Brandon was always there for her . . . until now.

"You know what I think, Angel?" Mic said, cutting through her mental debate when it was obvious she wasn't going to answer him. "I think you loved him, I really do. But I think you were wrapped up in the idea of loving him, the idea of someone loving you, the idea of a life with someone that you never really stopped to make sure was the one you wanted that life with. And I'm gonna tell you right now, you're fucking better than him."

He was right. She never stopped to really think if he was the one she wanted to spend the rest of her life with. She had just been with him for so long that she didn't know anything else. She did love him—they'd crawled their way up from the bottom of the barrel together—but if she was being fucking honest with herself, she wasn't *in* love with him—not anymore.

His betrayal is what hurt; it's what broke her heart, not the loss of his love but the loss of what his love represented. Safety.

"When did you get so philosophical?"

"Ah, when you are old like me you get a pretty good grasp at shit." Mic wasn't typically an affectionate man so when he reached out and pulled her into a hug it was awkward and uncomfortable, but it was just what she needed to break that ice that formed in her chest. He pulled away from her and when their eyes met, they both started rolling with laughter.

"Come on, Angel, we can finish my back another night. I think I have a bottle of Patrón stashed in the design room that is calling our name."

"I fucking love you," she said, and she followed him to the nice liquid that would dull her mind, and to the room that would only send her mind to thoughts of Kale.

EIGHT

The doorbell rang at twelve o'clock on the dot, right on time. Kale was either punctual or eager: either way, Ronnie liked it.

She opened the door and was surprised to see a gray Army sweatshirt and a worn pair of jeans on Kale. His face was scruffy, which she preferred, and a black beanie with the word Army across the front covered up his short high and tight haircut. This was the first time she had seen him in anything less than model-ready, but he was flirting with the line of sexy in an I-don't-have-to-try kind of way. He looked cozy and casual and damn it, he looked good.

"Would you like me to come in so you can undress me with your hands instead of your eyes?" Kale teased.

"Ha ha, funny. Let's go, smart-ass," she said, reaching for her coat that was on the bench in the entryway.

"You look beautiful by the way."

She looked down at her typical pants of choice, only these jeggins were a dark denim wash and her typical high-heeled pumps were replaced with a pair of black knee-high boots, and, yes, they were also high heels. Her top was a simple sheer black button-up blouse with a gold studded skull and angel wings on the back.

She didn't feel particularly beautiful today, especially after her internal emotional epiphany and the multiple shots of Patrón she went through last night, but her pulse sped up at his words just the same.

"Um, thanks."

Kale waited for Ronnie on the front patio while she locked up. She could feel him behind her and a part of her wanted to take him up on his offer and pull him in her house and undress him.

"Ready?" he asked when she slipped the keys into her purse. Was she ready for a four-hour road trip to visit his grandmother's grave just to turn around and drive four hours back? Fuck no. But for the first time in a long time, she held her tongue. She wanted to do this for him.

"Yep."

Kale opened the passenger-side door of a huge black truck and Ronnie was sure she was going to need a step stool to get into it. She eyed Kale as he stepped aside so she could climb in. She wouldn't have expected anything less than a gentleman from Captain America himself.

"How the fuck did I get into this damn thing the other night after I had been drinking?" She latched onto the "oh shit" handle and pulled herself up into the cab.

"It was quite entertaining," he chuckled, shutting the door, jogging around to the driver's side, and sliding in.

Ronnie looked down at the dark gray leather that

stretched between them, making the possibility of sliding over right next to him extremely easy. "Bench seat, huh?"

"I see where you mind is going." Kale lifted his lips in that sexy-ass smirk that drilled a dimple into his cheek. "All in good time, sweetheart, all in good time."

Yeah, right, if he kept looking at her like that, all in good time would turn into right now.

"You never told me where exactly we were going."

Kale started the truck, the engine roaring so loud she felt it rumble beneath her. "Montpelier."

"We're going to Vermont?"

"Yes, ma'am. To my hometown, born and raised." Kale fiddled with the heat dial as he pulled out on the road in front of her house. "You warm enough?"

"Yeah, I'm fine."

He looked over at her like he was checking to make sure there wasn't frost on her eyelashes or something. "Just turn it up or down if you need to."

Ronnie nodded. "It must be nice being only four hours from your family," she said, attempting to start up small talk, which was never her strong suit. She never usually cared enough to want to know anything about anyone, why she was starting now she didn't have a damn clue.

Kale pulled out of her neighborhood, heading toward the interstate. "I don't have any family, it's just me."

Dead. Silence. Ronnie knew a thing or two about not having anyone.

"Tell me about your grandmother," she said, trying to fill in the suffocating space of air that inhabited the cab of the truck.

"Well, she raised me. She was the only family I ever had growing up. My mom got pregnant with me when she was only seventeen; her family disowned her so she moved in with my dad and my grandmother."

"Wow. Seventeen." Ronnie knew plenty of girls who got pregnant at seventeen. Hell, her high school might as well have been a day care.

"Yeah, my grams said she was an amazing mom. My dad was amazing too. They died when I was two."

More silence. Ronnie was never good at condolences. She wasn't a compassionate person—she had enough in her own life to feel sorry for, she didn't need nor did she want to take on the shit storm of others'. But something in Kale's firm, strong voice tugged in her chest and she didn't know how to decipher it. She was suddenly more curious about this man.

"How did they die?"

"Car crash. My grams was watching me while my parents went to a movie. Some idiot ran a red light, slammed into my parents' car. Mom died instantly, and my dad died that night in the hospital."

"I'm sorry." And she truly was. He was dealt a pretty shitty hand himself.

"Don't be. I don't remember the loss. And I had my grams. She was a tough old lady. She raised my dad by herself, then got stuck raising my ass."

"She *must* have been pretty fucking tough then," Ronnie teased.

Kale looked over at her and his vulnerable expression

made her melt. He was so put-together all the time, so sure of himself. This little crack in his persona was refreshing.

He smiled at her. "She was amazing."

"So why the Army?" Ronnie was the queen of topic changes when it came to uncomfortable conversations, and getting all family-friendly was pushing her boundaries.

"I joined for college, well, with the intention of going to college. My grams couldn't afford to send me. I played sports in high school but I wasn't counting on getting any scholarships so I enlisted right after graduation. Grams was pissed too." His lips quirked up in a laugh like the memory was passing through his mind at that very moment. "Now I can't imagine doing anything else. I love my job and I love my platoon."

"Yeah, but what about all the deployments?"

"I'm not going to pretend like they're the icing on the cake or anything, but if it's where I'm needed, I'm there. I've got nothing here to miss, and my soldiers need me. I'm not doing them any good back here in the States. I have an obligation to them over there."

Ronnie couldn't believe he wanted to get back to Iraq, but it gave her a disquieting sense of pride. She couldn't wrap her head around it, but she knew that he was one of the good ones, and she knew they needed more men like him in the service.

She smiled at him, and she was sure that it looked every bit as cheesy as is felt. Fucking fantastic.

"What?" he asked, returning his own form of cheese, only his was flirting with seductive.

She peeled her eyes from him, not wanting to give away

her moment of admiration. "Nothing." Ronnie slipped out of her boots and propped her feet up on the dash as they pulled onto US-11. "So what's it like over there?"

"Like nothing you will see over here. It's miserable. The weather sucks ass, the food sucks ass, and no matter where you sleep or who you sleep next to, you never truly rest."

"What do you do?"

"Now who's writing a book?" Kale teased, although she got the impression that he was using banter to cover up the fact that he didn't really want to talk about it.

"Sorry. I'm just curious. You don't have to tell me," she said, and she was surprised by the sincerity in her words. She didn't want him to talk about his deployments if he wasn't up for it.

Kale sighed and his blue eyes went distant as he fixed his stare on the road ahead. Ronnie was pretty sure she was spot-on with her intuition and she regretted asking.

"Nah, it's okay. I'm a combat engineer. Each deployment has been a little different though. We go on missions every day, some may be a few hours and some may be a few days. Going outside the wire could be as simple of a mission as making a presence patrol, shaking hands with local civilians, and passing out candy to kids . . ."

Ronnie watched as Kale took in a deep breath, seemingly lost in thought. His eyes turned to hers for the briefest of moments but it was long enough for her to see the myriad of emotions swirling beneath them—anger and pride, pain and loss, honor and determination—it was like watching a funnel cloud form in clear blue skies.

"And in the blink of an eye the mission can turn into house raids and body bags." His hands tightened on the steering wheel and the muscles in his jaw clenched as he swallowed hard.

Ronnie thought back to the beautiful prayer she tattooed on his back.

And may my fallen brothers
Walk with you now, Lord.

She knew he was talking about them, the three men whose names she forever embedded into his flesh.

"Kale," she said softly, unsure of where she was going with this, but she knew she had to say something.

He shifted his eyes to her, never fully turning his head to look at her, but still letting her know he was listening.

Ronnie did something completely out of character, completely shocking the hell out of her, and something so out of line with their little arrangement that she prayed she wouldn't regret it later. Unbuckling her seat belt, she slid across the seat until her thigh was pressed up against Kale's. The instant her body touched his, she saw him physically relax. He exhaled a breath that she wasn't aware he'd been holding and his shoulders rolled forward. She knew in that moment that even though she hated letting even a fleck of the minuscule soft side that she possessed inside her slip through, she wouldn't regret it.

She grabbed his right hand, peeling it from his grip on the steering wheel, and kissed the inside of his palm. "I'm sorry," she whispered, and then she kissed his palm again.

She released his hand and instead of placing it back on the steering wheel, he slipped it through her hair and ran his thumb over her cheekbone. "Thank you," he whispered, and the look he was giving her had her hard interior momentarily turning to putty; and just like that she slid back on over to her side of the truck.

Kale immediately missed the warmth of Ronnie sitting next to him. She wasn't there for more the sixty seconds but the brief touch left him with phantom sensations along the places where their bodies met. He wanted to reach over and pull her back to him, but she would have stayed there if she wanted to, and she didn't.

The rest of the drive went by in silence. What with the heavy burden of Kale's past lingering in the air between them, there wasn't much to be said. Before he knew it Ronnie had her head leaned against the window with her eyes shut and her feet propped back up on the dash—she was asleep.

"I can feel you staring at me," she said as Kale took the ramp from I-89 to the Montpelier exit a few hours later.

"I thought you were still sleeping."

Ronnie's lids fluttered open, her brown eyes blinking to life. "Is this it?" She sat up and looked out the passenger window as he turned onto Memorial Drive toward downtown. He was home.

"Yep."

"Huh," she sighed, her words giving a verbal shrug.

"What was the 'huh' for?"

She leaned forward and yanked on her boots. "I didn't expect it to be so . . . cozy."

"Cozy?"

She rolled her eyes at him. "Just pull in somewhere, I'm about to pee my pants."

"Well, we definitely wouldn't want that." Kale pulled into the next gas station and drove up to the pump. He watched as Ronnie hopped out and gracefully power walked to the doors. How she managed to move so fast in heels was lost on him, but he sure as shit enjoyed watching.

Kale was just topping off the tank when Ronnie appeared on the other side of the truck bed holding a bag of Sour Patch Kids and a Snickers in one hand and two Big Gulp sodas tucked tightly in her other arm.

"Sour Patch Kids? What are you, ten?"

"Kiss my ass, Emerson," she spat.

"Gladly, sweetheart." He curved his lips in the way he knew would get a reaction from her, and it worked. Ronnie chucked the Snickers at him, hitting him in the chest before it dropped to his hands.

"Don't say I never gave you anything," she hissed before hopping back in the truck.

Kale shook his head and laughed under his breath as he put the cap back on his gas tank. He stepped into the cab, Ronnie sending him a narrow-eyed glare, and he ripped open the Snickers, taking half of it in his mouth in one bite. He nodded his head and smiled. "Thanks, baby," he said around a mouth full of nuts and chocolate. Then he pulled back out onto the road.

A few minutes later, they were pulling into the cemetery. Kale hadn't been back to visit his grandmother's grave since the day after they put her in the ground, the day he'd had to leave to go back to Fort Hood where he was stationed at the time. Her headstone hadn't even been up yet. That was three years ago.

He parked on the side of the road that tangled in all directions around the cemetery. He took a deep breath and pulled the bouquet of lilies he had tucked away before they left out of the backseat. Lilies were his grams's favorite.

"I'll be back in a few, I won't take too long." He opened the door and before he got one foot out of the truck Ronnie was opening her door too.

"I'll go with you."

"You don't have to—"

"I want to," she said, hopping out and shutting the door before Kale had another chance to object. He walked around the truck and stood in front of her.

"Are you sure?"

"Yeah, I want to pay my respects to the woman who raised you"—her eyes held his and her expression was gentle and sweet, nothing like the way she usually looked at him—"even if you are a huge pain in the ass."

"I will take that as a compliment coming from you."

"Yeah, well, don't get used to it. I'm in rare form today."

"I've noticed." He reached forward and grabbed her hand, lacing his fingers through hers. She looked down at their joined hands and then back to him. He could see the indecision cross over her face, her forehead wrinkling between her eyes, and he pulled her closer to him, walking away from the truck before she had the chance to decide against it.

Kale walked to the spot where his grandmother's grave was, never once needing to look around to make sure he was in the right section. He may have only been there the two times after she passed, but it was embedded in his memory. She lay right next to his mother and father. The sad things are always harder to forget.

They came to a large headstone, one Kale had carefully picked out himself. It was a beautifully marbleized soft gray stone with a photo of his grandmother when she was twenty-five etched in the front above the words that, until now, Kale had never seen.

Marilyn Emerson
Her body lies to rest beneath the ground,
her soul walks eternally with the Lord,
and her memory lives forever in our hearts.

Kale felt Ronnie's fingers tighten around his hand. "She was beautiful."

"That she was," Kale said, reading over the words a second time. He let go of Ronnie and stepped forward, laying the lilies down on the frozen ground next to the stone. "Hey, Grams," he whispered. "Sorry it's taken me so long to get back here. I miss you." He pulled a single lily from the bouquet, stood up and backed away, needing a little distance to calm the burn in the back of his throat.

Whoever said it got easier with time was wrong: death never got easier. The pain dulled around your heart, numbing the spot the deceased inhabited in your chest—but it was never easier. Loss was still loss—a physical pain, a hurt that reached deep inside you and smothered your soul, forever indenting their memory. No, death was still death, loss was still loss, and pain was still pain. Time didn't change that.

He took the small step to the side and stood in front of his mother and father's headstone, laying the single flower on top. Kale lifted his hands out in front of him and gestured to the three graves before them. "This is my family." This was it, this was everyone that had ever meant anything to him, and they were all here . . . gone.

They stood there in silence together for an endless amount of time that was measured in only a matter of a few minutes, but it was just long enough to mend the ache that swept over him since the moment he pulled into the cemetery.

The atmosphere in the car as they left the cemetery and headed back into town was thick and more than a little stiff, making Kale wonder whether or not he made the right decision bringing Ronnie.

"You kind of look like her, ya know?" Her words sliced through the small space in the truck.

"What?" Kale asked, pulling himself out of his own head.

"Your grams—you have her eyes."

Kale turned to look at her but her face was toward the

window, hiding any vulnerable emotion she was having from him.

Kale pulled into the parking lot of a large brick building that was overrun by cars. This place was packed, as usual. They had the best pizza in town. Kale had come here every week growing up. They were famous for their homemade pizza pies and beer. They had their own microbrewery and their own brand of beer. It was hands down the best beer Kale had ever had. The owners had had several offers to go mainstream with their brand but they refused to sell. If you want their beer, you gotta get it here.

"What is this place?" Ronnie asked as Kale parked the truck.

He turned off the engine and tucked the keys in his pocket. "I hope you're hungry."

"You did this on purpose, didn't you?"

"What, offer to feed you? Yes, I did that on purpose. Look, Ronnie, it's just pizza. Loosen up, sweetheart."

"But—"

"Stay in the truck if you want but I'm gonna get some food." He got out and walked to the passenger door, opening it for Ronnie. "You coming?"

Ronnie just rolled her eyes and got out of the truck.

"Good girl."

Ronnie pinned him with a look that made him laugh and cringe at the same time. "Watch it, soldier."

They stepped into the restaurant; warm air filled with the aroma of fresh-baked bread filled their noses. "Fuck, is the whole damn town here or something?" Ronnie asked, looking around at the crowded room of people chatting and stuffing their faces.

"Pretty much; come on." Kale led Ronnie into the restaurant, scanning the area for an open table when a voice thundered from across the room.

"No freakin' way! Kale Emerson?" Kale turned toward the voice in time to see a short, overly round guy approaching with a cheese-eatin' grin on his face.

"Fat Andy!" Kale said, hugging the guy.

"Emerson. What the hell, buddy! I haven't seen you in years. How the hell you been? Last I heard you were fighting over in Iraq."

"I am. I'm home on R and R; I just drove up to visit Grams."

Andy nodded his head with a knowing look before turning his attention to Ronnie, who was cautiously watching their little reunion.

"And where did you pick up this lovely lady?" he asked, not trying to hide his wandering eyes, as he looked Ronnie up and down.

"She—" Kale started but Ronnie stepped closer to Andy and finished his sentence for him.

"He didn't pick me up anywhere, and I'm no lady. People really need to stop fucking calling me that. The name's Ronnie."

Instead of being taken back by Ronnie's bite-your-head-off response, Andy just shook with laughter. "Oh I like this one, Emerson. Feisty. You'd better hold on to her."

Kale met eyes with Ronnie. Yeah, he was kind of thinking the same thing.

"Come on, man, Matt's here, and Trisha and Cammie are meeting us up here later. Come sit with us, it'll be like old times."

Kale waited to see how Ronnie responded. He didn't want to throw her into a situation where she was forced to meet some of his high school buddies. He knew that didn't fall into the terms of their arrangement. Hell, he was just glad she came inside with him. He didn't want to push his luck.

"I don't care where we sit as long as someone feeds me, and soon," Ronnie said, filling in the awkward silence.

Andy cocked his head to the side. "The lady has spoken. Come on, Ronnie, let Fat Andy show you how pizza is done here in Montpelier."

Kale was relieved when Ronnie just smiled and followed.

Before he knew it almost two hours had passed. Ronnie impressively consumed damn near an entire pizza all by herself and had been working her magic busting his buddies' balls and drinking beer like a grown man. It made her even sexier, if that was even possible.

"I'm going to need to get a keg of this beer to go. Seriously, Kale, this is fucking amazing. Mic would go ape-shit," she said, setting down her empty glass.

"Told ya, sweetheart."

Ronnie stood up, wobbling a little in her heels but she recovered quickly. "You up for a game of darts?"

Kale stood up next to her and leaned his head down close to her ear. "Are you ready to get your ass handed to you?"

She turned her head to the side so she was looking at his eyes, heat turning her brown eyes into smoldering chocolate. "Depends on who's doing the handing," she said, insinuating things Kale had been dreaming up in his mind since he first touched her body.

His eyes went cloudy and his voice got low. "Oh, that most definitely will be me."

"Then I'm most definitely ready."

"Are we going to get some more beer and play some darts, or are you two going to stand there and give each other sex eyes all night?"

"Screw you, Andy," Kale said, never taking his gaze from Ronnie.

Ronnie tore her eyes from him and fixed them on Andy. "Emerson here is just procrastinating, putting off the inevitable outcome of failure."

Fat Andy came around and gripped Kale on the shoulder. "Sounds like you've got yourself a challenge there, little buddy."

"That I do," he said to himself as he watched Ronnie's hips rock in rhythm to the click of her heels as she headed to the back of the bar—and he was definitely up for the challenge.

A couple rounds later and with only a slight bruise to his ego, Kale sat at the table watching this sexy woman with complete amusement.

"Oh, yeah!" Ronnie slurred as she walked back to the table after annihilating Matt in a game of darts. She was slightly past tipsy and was toying with drunk but she was cute as hell. "Who wants to try their luck against me next?" Ronnie was showing them all up, kicking their sorry asses one by one.

"How the hell did you get so good at darts?" Matt asked, looking like a kid who just got his candy taken away from him.

Ronnie just laughed and shook her head at him. "Sorry, buddy. I've been around more beer-drinking, dart-throwing men in my lifetime than I can count. And on top of that my best friend, Mic, and I play every Friday night so I've had a lot of practice."

Matt wrapped his arm around her shoulders and pulled her into a headlock/hug. "Well, looks like I'm buying the next round. Be right back."

Just as Matt released Ronnie from his big brother–like embrace, a couple of girls walked in, one girl in particular pointing her pissed-off eyes at Ronnie, obviously not missing their hug.

"Is it just me or am I getting the stink eye from Barbie over there?" Ronnie asked loud enough for everyone around them to hear, and Kale knew that was her full intention.

Matt returned with four glasses of beer wedged between his hands. "Here ya go."

"Hey, baby," the blonde said, making her way to Matt as he set the beers down on the table. She wrapped her arms around his waist, never taking her eyes off Ronnie. Leave it to Trisha to be full of girl drama.

Luckily, Kale didn't think Ronnie seemed too bothered by Trisha; if anything she seemed amused.

Obviously, Trisha thought the same thing. "What's so funny?" Trisha asked as Ronnie shook her head and laughed.

"You are."

"Matt, who is this?" Trisha asked, spitting deadly venom at Ronnie.

"This is Kale's girl."

"I'm not—"

"Kale!!" A voice squealed from behind Trisha, interrupting Ronnie. Kale was all too familiar with that high-pitched sound. Hell, it had haunted his dreams his entire senior year of high school. That's what he got for sleeping with a cheerleader.

A short, voluptuous brunette came into view right as her arms wound around his neck. If it weren't for Andy mentioning that Cammie was going to be coming up here, he would have never recognized her apart from her voice. Her hair was cut short and sleek to her chin and her figure was fuller and curvier. She was a knock-out in high school but now she was downright sexy.

"Hey, Cammie." He awkwardly hugged her back. He could see Ronnie out of the corner of his eye and her lips pressed into a line, suppressing a laugh. He was starting to understand why she didn't have many girlfriends. The woman was not female friendly.

Cammie pulled away from him and looked at him like she was admiring a rare, lost artifact. "I can't believe you are here! Jeez, how long has it been? Two years?"

"Three."

"It's so good to see you. I've missed you."

"You too, Cam," he said softly. He looked over at Ronnie who was just watching them impassively, her smirk no longer sneaking to the surface.

The women sat down at a table next to them and it was Kale's turn to suppress his laugh as he watched them glower at Ronnie as she went about her way and returned to giving his buddies a hard time. Ronnie didn't even give them a second glance. She didn't take shit from anyone, and she sure as hell wasn't going to let those females intimidate her either.

Kale turned his head away from the table in time to see the looming figure of a beefed-up, shaggy-headed douche bag making his way toward their table. "Fuck, Andy. Is anyone else planning on making an appearance that I should know about?" Kale asked between clenched teeth as he made eye contact with Mason Muller, a walking piece of shit who ran his mouth and treated women like cheap whores.

Kale and Mason had had a few run-ins back in school. The guy was bad news and Kale never had much tolerance for bottom feeders with an agenda. Mason was the epitome of a womanizer.

Mason's eyes trailed from Kale to Ronnie, and Kale watched as his lips slowly lifted at the corners. Kale instantly stepped closer to her. He knew Ronnie wouldn't give that piece of shit the time of day, but that didn't mean that Mason wouldn't try.

Ronnie could obviously hold her own and he knew good and well that she would never fall for his sleazy act, but he couldn't help the urge that swept through him as Mason got closer to them. He took the final step that separated him from Ronnie and grabbed her hand. He moved his eyes over hers, knowing that his little public display of affection would probably roil her; but she didn't jerk away or lash out, or spit out some "fuck you" comment. She just offered him a slight smile; and it was fucking beautiful.

"Looks like I picked the perfect night to come out for pizza," Mason said when he approached the table. Cammie and Trisha eyed Kale suspiciously; they obviously remembered how he felt about Mason.

"Mason," Kale said calmly, evenly, yet a threat saturated the single word as it left his lips.

"Well, if it isn't Army boy," Mason replied, and Kale felt Ronnie's hand flex in his and he knew she was biting her tongue.

Mason slowly and purposefully licked his lips as he nodded his head at Ronnie. "Hey," he said with what Kale assumed Mason thought was a smooth greeting. Little did Mason know just what kind of a woman he was pressing his luck with.

Ronnie laughed at Mason's attempt at whatever the hell he was attempting, and it was a low and luscious sound. Then just like that, she turned it off and snapped her eyes at Mason, making him blink in surprise. "Hey your-fucking-self," she spat.

All eyes flashed in surprise at Ronnie. Not too many women had the balls to talk to Mason like that, but not too many women were like Ronnie either.

Mason nodded his head up and down in approval. "Ah, sexy and mouthy, I like it."

Kale moved Ronnie slightly behind him, keeping her hand secured tightly in his. Kale didn't get worked up easily but it was taking everything he had in him not to swing at this asshole and Ronnie's hand in his was a small preventative.

He gritted his teeth together. "You need to back off, Mason."

"I need to back off?" Mason laughed, and the sound ran through Kale's ears like nails on a chalkboard. "What are you doing with a sweet little piece of ass like her anyway?" He lifted his hands out in front of him, gesturing toward Ronnie. "This bad girl needs a man who can handle her."

Kale's previously level head tipped the scale and teetered over to losing it when he felt Ronnie's body tense behind him. In one quick graceful movement, Kale slipped his hand from Ronnie's and clocked Mason in the jaw, spinning him to the ground. Kale leaned over him and grabbed ahold of his shirt, lifting Mason's head slightly off the ground.

Leaning in close so he was nose to nose with him, Kale whispered so only Mason could hear, "First of all, you need to watch your fucking mouth. Second, that sweet little piece of bad-girl ass, as you like to call her, is mine." Kale swung his fist back around and it connected with Mason's face again, dropping his head back to the hard floor.

Kale stood up, keeping his back to Ronnie and his friends. He had no claim over Ronnie, she wasn't his, and he was afraid to see what look was waiting for him in her eyes . . .

He was pleasantly surprised when he turned around and saw her hand hoisted up on her hip and a plausive smile forming on her lips. She surprised him again when she grabbed her purse and stepped around the table to him, grabbing his hand.

Kale drank her in, the high of his adrenaline still swimming in his head. Finally, he leaned down and whispered, "Ready to go?"

She looked up at him through her lashes and she didn't say a word, just winked. That was all it took for him to pull her through the bar and through the parking lot. Neither one said anything until they were in the car and pulling onto the road.

Ronnie leaned back against the seat. "Are you sure you are okay to drive? I for one was enjoying that beer a little too much. I'm going to have to make monthly trips down here now, thanks to you."

"Don't come without me."

"Why?"

"Just don't. Mason isn't known for his ability to take a hint from a woman and after what happened back there, he would be all too eager to attempt something on you. So don't come here without me."

"He could try all he wants but—"

"Ronnie, please." Kale knew the reputation Mason had was based off a lot more than just rumors, and the thought of Mason being near Ronnie was enough to make him see red.

"Okay. I was just kidding anyway. I have no intention to drive four hours for beer."

Kale sighed as his body relaxed and the crimson haze cleared from his vision. "I'm sorry about grabbing onto you back there." That wasn't true. He wasn't sorry. He would never be sorry for holding that woman close to him if she let him.

"I can tell a testosterone pissing match when I see one. It was no problem." She winked and he knew then that she only had done it so Kale could send his message to Mason. Who was he kidding? Ronnie would have loved to lash out at that piece of shit; he knew she was holding back. She was playing along.

A stab in his chest shot like a hundred tiny daggers. She hadn't let him hold on to her and pull her to his side because she wanted him to; she was just playing along.

"Nice right hook by the way. Very hot if I do say so," Ronnie said, slipping out of her boots. Kale smiled and winked at her, pushing aside his mental run-through.

"Holy shit, it's already nine. How long were we there for?" Ronnie mumbled.

Kale laughed as her words slurred. Normally girls this drunk annoyed the shit out of him, but with Ronnie, it was rather amusing. "Almost four hours."

"Well, shit. You never answered me. Are you okay to drive?"

"Yes, sweetheart. I only had three beers and it takes a lot more than that to affect me."

"Okay good, because I'm just going to lay my head down right here"—she unbuckled her seat belt and laid her head down on the bench seat next to Kale's lap—"and I'm going to take a little nap."

He lifted his hand and ran his fingers through her hair. "You do that, baby."

"Mmm," she moaned, closing her eyes and pulling her legs up on the seat so she was curled into a ball next to him.

Her blouse pulled up when she tucked her arms under her head and the sweet soft skin of her side was making an appearance, showing off her delicate tattoo that traveled down the side of her body. He wanted to move his fingers down to skim over the soft flesh on her side but he didn't. He kept his fingers working through her hair, brushing her temple with his thumb. She sighed and tucked in tighter to herself, letting little moans of satisfaction roll off her lips.

"This isn't part of our arrangement, but I'm going to let it slide," she said, and Kale decided touching her like this, making her sigh and moan, and making her body relax under his fingertips, was even better.

NINE

Ronnie woke up as the truck pulled to a stop. She kept her eyes closed, wishing they were still driving so she wouldn't have to move. She felt a hand run over the top of her head, down her neck and to her back, softly jostling her until her eyes opened.

"Hey," Kale whispered. He rubbed his hand softly over her back and she laid there for a second longer relishing the roughness of his fingertips brushing the sheer fabric of her blouse. The two textures caused a friction that felt amazing. "Sorry to wake you up, but you're home."

Ronnie groaned as she pushed herself up, causing Kale's hand to drop to the side. "I can't believe I slept the whole way. Sorry I wasn't much of a road-trip partner." She yawned and reached down to grab her boots, not even bothering with putting them on.

"Don't worry about it. Come on, let's get you to bed, lush."

"Oh what the fuck ever. I didn't drink that much."

Kale raised his eyebrows in speculation of her idea of what constituted "that much."

Ronnie frowned. "Yeah, you're right."

Kale just laughed and got out of the car, walking around to open the door for her.

She hopped out and walked to her front door, digging in her purse for her keys as Kale followed next to her. "Damn it."

"What?"

"I think I left my phone in the cup holder in your truck. I don't see it in my purse," she said, unlocking the door.

"I'll go check."

Kale turned and jogged back toward the truck and Ronnie pushed open the door. The warm air inside the house wrapped around her cold body when she walked inside. She dropped her purse and boots by the door and headed straight for her bedroom. She wanted to get out of her clothes and into her sweats so she could curl up in bed and pass out. For some unknown reason, car trips made her exhausted, apparently even if she slept the whole damn time.

Ronnie peeled off her jeans, stepping out of them and kicking them to the side when she heard the front door shut. "Help yourself to whatever," she hollered to Kale. "I will be right there." She unbuttoned her blouse, letting it drop to the ground, and gasped when she felt the lightest of touches trace over her back.

She froze, letting every nerve ending fire to life as Kale's fingers traced over the lines of her tattoo. The softness of his touch was so light, so careful, it was as if she was feeling the light pressure of a needle pressing ink into her skin. It was like he was tattooing her body all over again with the tip of his finger, and the feeling was addictive. She wanted more, and she wanted it everywhere.

His lips came down and closed on her shoulder, pressing featherlight kisses to her now heated skin. His hand was gently running down her arm, now following the directions of the tattoos trickling down her shoulder to her elbow, sending goose bumps cascading in every direction. His body pressed against her back and she could feel his bare chest warm against her.

It was hard and inviting and she welcomed the feel of it as his weight crushed into her, his stomach molding into the dip in her back. His lips slowly found their way to her neck, taking their time getting there, kissing and licking her tender skin along the way. Ronnie tilted her head to the side, laying it back so it rested on his shoulder. He ran both hands down her arms, stopping as they tickled her palms, and then he laced his fingers through hers, continuing to set flames to her skin. The way he touched her was so sincere that it made her heart ache like it was breaking into a thousand pieces at the same time that it was gluing it back together.

She tightened her hands in his, turning her head slightly more to the side. He lifted his head from her neck and his eyes homed in on hers. They were flooded with need—raw, hungry, intense need—and it terrified her.

Kale dropped one of Ronnie's hands and spun her around, pulling her body flush against his. "I've been dying to touch you all day," he whispered, trailing a single finger up her spine. The touch was so light, the sensation was almost unbearable. When it reached her bra, he unsnapped it in one single flick. He slowly pushed the straps down her shoulders, like he was savoring every single inch as it fell down her arms, before he let it drop to the floor.

"I'm gonna kiss you now, okay?" His voice was hushed and low, as if he didn't know what answer he was going to get.

Ronnie could only nod like a dumbfounded idiot. He had her in a trance. His hands and his eyes locked her in an intimacy that she was petrified of, yet she wanted it more than she had ever wanted anything. She wanted him more than she has ever wanted anyone.

"Are you sure?" he asked carefully, his lips only a breath away from connecting to hers.

Why was he asking her if she was sure? He never asked for her permission before. But even as the question ran through her mind, she had the answer. This was different, he knew it and she knew it. It felt different. Not just the way he touched her, or the way he looked at her, because those were different now too, but more than that, it was the way she felt when he touched her. It didn't just make her insides shudder and tighten, or make her pulse race. Now it made a fluttering sensation gather in her chest, it made her throat constrict, and it scared the living hell out of her.

He remained still, his mouth hovering over hers, his fingers kneading her knuckles softly as he kept ahold of her hand. He grasped her chin and held her head firmly in place as he raised his gaze to her eyes.

"Ronnie?" he asked, his eyes forming clouds like a deadly thunderstorm reaching the horizon.

Seeing him so gentle with her, so concerned, was almost too much to bear, but regardless, she only had this man for a few more days and she wasn't going to waste them contemplating soft touches and intimate looks. No, she was going to just feel; just like he told her to on Valentine's Day. Just feel, and right now she just wanted to feel him—against her, on her, inside her, all of it.

"I'm sure," she said, and before the word finished bouncing through the sliver of air between them, he kissed her.

His lips were soft and easy, like no kiss she had ever shared with him. It was powerful and overwhelming and possessing. His mouth moved over hers with purpose, slowly and carefully dripping everything he had into her, like he was giving her a piece of him; and she willingly took it.

Her hands trailed up his naked chest and wrapped around the back of his neck. He moaned in her mouth as she pressed her nails into his flesh, bringing him closer to her.

Kale wrapped his arms around her waist and lifted her feet off the ground, carrying her to her bed. He slowly lowered her, never once taking his mouth off hers.

When he finally pulled his lips away, she watched him as he leaned over her, pulling her lace panties down her legs, and over her ankles, dropping them to the floor with the remainder of her clothing. She leaned up on her elbows so she could see the full length of him as he stood up and stepped out of his jeans and boxers.

"God, you're perfect," he said, inching his eyes up her body.

She could most definitely say the same thing about him.

Without saying another word, Kale carefully rolled on a condom and climbed on the bed, hovering between her legs.

She needed his mouth on hers, she needed to taste him, to get lost in his touch, because getting lost in his stare felt too dangerous. She pressed her lips to his and waited for him to reciprocate. It took him a single heartbeat but then he kissed her. He kissed her like it was the first time, hungry and passionate; spewing nothing but raw desire. But he also kissed her with such longing that it felt like it was the last time, intense and desperate.

All the conflicting emotions were thudding against Ronnie's already tender heart, bruising it and healing it only to repeat the torture over again, and she didn't know if she could handle it.

It was as if Kale read her mind; it was like he knew exactly what she needed to bury the thoughts, to drown the feelings that were crawling their way to the surface. He tucked his hand under her and rolled over onto his back, pulling her on top of him. His erection was against her ass and Kale grabbed her hips, lifting her and rolling her back, until she felt him beneath her. She slowly lowered herself, feeling inch by every delicious inch of him as he filled her body, stretching her around him.

"God, baby," he said, digging his fingers into her thighs as she sank all the way down on top of him. "Come here."

He tangled his fingers in her hair and pulled her down on top of him. Her chest collapsed on top of his, every part of her body touching him. She rocked back slowly, letting his length slide almost completely out of her before she rolled her hips forward, swallowing him deep inside her. His lips crushed hers, his teeth nipping her bottom lip and his tongue swiping across it soothingly. His hands roamed over her waist, her back, her breasts, and everywhere in between. They were exploring her with such tenderness that it made her skin tingle with shooting pricks of pleasure that radiated throughout her body, piling up where their bodies were most connected.

In a movement so fluid that she didn't register it until it was over, Kale had her underneath him. He was still inside of her and his body took over the rocking. Ronnie hooked her feet around his calves, anchoring her so she could roll her hips and meet him thrust for thrust.

His big body was pressing her into the mattress as his lips continued moving against hers, making her light-headed as she struggled to pull air into her lungs, but being so consumed by Kale that she became breathless was a feeling she invited completely.

As his hips moved slowly in a circle, a tingling pleasure started building and building between her thighs. Kale seemed to notice her body quickening and shuddering and he slowly started picking up his speed, yet he remained completely gentle. Every thrust sent her further until she couldn't hold on any longer. And then she let go. She let go of her mind and her body and she just felt, and it was amazing. Kale's perfect lips softly caressed hers as a delicious spasm rippled through her core. She moaned into his mouth, causing a sexy groan in response as she felt Kale's pleasure pumping into her.

He stilled inside her and planted featherlight kisses to her lips, jaw and neck.

"That was amazing," Ronnie said breathlessly as Kale continued to tend to her sensitive skin.

"That it was," he whispered, and she could feel him smile against the side of her neck.

Kale rolled off her and pulled her into his arms. She almost hesitated, but didn't. She was exhausted, her body was still spiraling back down, and she just didn't have the fucking energy to protest. Yeah, that's what she kept telling herself. It was better than admitting that the feeling of being cradled in his strong arms felt better than anything else had in a really long time.

Kale's mind slowly and groggily shifted back into the territory of awake as morning crept through the windows, but he wasn't quite ready to open his eyes. He took a deep breath and tightened his arms around Ronnie. She was still wrapped around him, her limbs tangling with his naked skin. She was so light and soft, and she was actually sweet while she was sleeping, something that would only be true about this woman while she was asleep.

He carefully slipped his body out from under hers, trying not to wake her up as he climbed out of the bed. He looked down at her, her creamy ivory skin covered in colorful art, her long, almost-black hair spilling out around her head onto the pillow, her pouty lips parted slightly, her long lashes brushing the tops of her cheeks. She was breathtakingly beautiful.

Kale quietly stepped into the bathroom and turned on the shower. When he stepped in his eyes immediately zoomed in on the caddy containing men's body wash, men's shaving cream, and a man's razor—and it pissed him off to no end. He almost forgot that Ronnie had shared her life with someone; that she at one point in time wasn't afraid of love and of everything that came along with it.

For the first time ever, Kale thought about what it would be like to have this woman every day, forever. He thought about what it would be like to sleep next to her every night, to make love to her anytime she wanted him to, to rub her feet and to kiss her neck and for the first time since he had been in the Army, he wanted to stay. Did he still want to be with his men? Absolutely. But for the first time, something mattered more to him than the mission.

He didn't want to leave; he didn't want to leave Ronnie. He finally understood the cost, and it was worse than he ever could have imagined.

Kale turned off the shower once the water was no longer warm. He quickly dressed back in his clothes and walked out of the now empty bedroom. As he rounded the corner from the hallway, he saw Ronnie standing in the kitchen making breakfast. She was wearing a tiny tank top and leopard print panties. He knew they were called boy shorts but they sure as hell didn't look like anything a boy would wear. They barely covered her ass, not that he was complaining, and they set so low on her hips it wouldn't take much for him to push them down just a tad and he could . . .

"Pancakes?" Ronnie asked, meeting his eyes as he

plopped down at the bar. She pranced around the counter and stopped right next to him, setting down a mound of pancakes.

"Yes, ma'am." He grabbed her by the waist and pulled her onto his lap, and planted a quick kiss on her neck. She felt a little uncomfortable there, like it was forced, so he let her go, a sinking feeling taking over his stomach.

"So what's on the agenda today?" he asked, slathering peanut butter on his stack of pancakes, pushing aside the feelings that were sure to take away his man card.

"Well, I have a full schedule at the shop and then I'm supposed to meet Jordan for drinks later. What about you?"

"I have some shit to take care of for work before I head back to the sandpit."

The look that flashed over Ronnie's eyes was brief and he didn't get the chance to figure out what it was before they hardened again.

Two more days, he only had two more days with her.

"Well, help yourself to whatever. I'm going to jump in the shower and get ready for work. I will call you tomorrow?"

When did the roles reverse? When did he suddenly become the one being rushed off in the mornings?

"Yep," he said before cramming his mouth full of pancakes. He smiled and winked in her general direction but didn't meet her eyes. He was afraid they would say what he knew good and well they would—it was just sex.

Only now, it was so much more than that.

TEN

"Good morning, Angel," Mic said as Ronnie walked into the shop. He was leaning against the reception desk, his eyelids barely lifted.

Ronnie laughed and patted Mic on the shoulder as she passed him. "It's twelve thirty in the afternoon. What are you doing up so early?"

Mic followed Ronnie down the hall to the design room, his heavy steps dragging behind her. "Harold needed me to open up for him this morning, something to do with being in the doghouse with the wife."

Ronnie laughed again. "I wonder what he did now."

"What is with the chipper attitude this morning?"

She flung her purse down on the design table and turned to look at her overweight, balding, pain-in-the-ass friend, who had now taken up the couch as his bed. "I didn't realize I was being chipper."

"Laughter isn't usually in your typical workday routine, Angel. There's a reason for that shit-eatin' grin on your face." He laid on his own grin and Ronnie felt her face flush.

She knew the reason her mood was in rare form, and the realization of that alone was enough to make her heart skip a beat, and it scared her.

The memory of Kale's long fingers gripping her waist and pulling her onto his lap this morning ran through the cloudy space of her mind. Her body felt right against his, even in the casual, playful way he had pulled her to him at breakfast—but her mind had slammed on the brakes before his impact could affect her. She refused to let herself go there. Kale was a soldier, and he was leaving in two days. It was just sex; it had to be just sex.

"Ah, did someone have a good night last night?" Mic asked, sitting up on the couch.

Ronnie rolled her eyes in an attempt to bury the debate her mind and body were having. "My night was fine," she said, her words clipped.

"And I'm guessing by the sudden mood swing that your night was spent with a certain soldier." Mic patted the spot next to him on the couch. "Come talk to me, Angel."

Ronnie shook her head, exasperated, but a slight smile pulled on her lips as she crossed the room to the couch and sat down next to Mic. She slipped her heels off and tucked her feet up to her side.

"So what, we have a heart-to-heart the other night and now you think I'm just gonna spill my guts to you every time I have a moment?"

"I sure do. Now what's going in that beautifully demented mind of yours?"

"Oh my God, we are not having this conversation," she

said through a deep sigh, leaning her head back against the cold leather of the couch.

Mic's deep smoker's laugh erupted through the room. "Let me take a swing at it, can I?"

Ronnie lifted her head and arched her brows.

"So, I'm assuming you took my advice and let that soldier get you back on the horse."

"Seriously?" Ronnie asked, letting her head fall back against the couch again.

"And that would be a yes," Mic laughed. "Good. You needed a distraction from Brandon. You deserve to let loose a little."

A chill worked its way through Ronnie's chest as she thought of last night, as she thought of the way Kale's lips had skimmed over her shoulder and up the side of her neck.

"That was the easy part," she whispered.

Mic leaned toward her. "And there's a hard part, I take it?"

Ronnie inhaled a deep breath, her lungs filling up to capacity, causing her chest to expand before she loudly huffed out the air through her lips. "There is always a hard part."

"Ah, your body's not the only thing he's gotten into, is it?"

"Mic!" she shouted as she slapped him on the arm. "You did not just fucking say that to me." She stood up off the couch, suddenly annoyed with the direction this conversation was going.

"You like him, Angel. What's the big deal?"

Mic's words stalled her steps. She stood there with her back to him, slowly pulling oxygen in through her nose in hopes to calm the feelings that were erratically forming in her chest.

She shifted around to face him, her eyes locking with Mic's as she tried to convince herself as well as him. "I don't."

"It's okay to go there, ya know. No one is going to hold anything against you if you break down that fucking wall you built up. It might do you some good." Mic sprawled back out on the couch, his hands resting behind his head.

She leaned down and picked up her heels. "It might do you some good to stay awake while the sun is out," she said, easily changing the subject as she always did.

"What fun would that be?" he asked as he yawned and stretched.

Ronnie rolled her eyes and slipped on her heels. "I'm ordering Chinese takeout for lunch, you want some?" she asked as she walked toward the door.

"You know it."

"The usual?"

"Yep."

Ronnie walked out of the design room and headed back toward the front room to order lunch before her first appointment got there. The door chimed as someone walked into the shop, just as she was hanging up the phone.

"Well, first time's a charm. You weren't so hard to find after all." The sound of the unfamiliar voice brought a fuzzy image to her mind in the quick second before her eyes focused in on his face. Mason.

His hair fell across his forehead, brushing the tops of his eyes, but it didn't veil the dark, insidious look that ringed them. The corners of his mouth slowly pulled up, and the hair on the back of Ronnie's neck prickled at the expression that lined his face.

"What do you want?" Ronnie bit out between clenched teeth.

"I wanted to pay a visit to the sexy bad girl that stirred up the all-American hometown hero." He flexed his jaw and Ronnie saw the slight bruising that was forming below his cheek.

"You drove over four hours because you're pissed about a little punch to the face? Seriously, man, you need to grow a pair," Ronnie said, narrowing her eyes at him while she kept herself planted behind the reception desk, keeping herself separated from Mason.

A chuckle that sounded like it belonged to a cartoon character villain rolled from his mouth. "I'm more than pissed, and I saw something I liked." He paused, his eyebrows twitching up as he scanned the length of Ronnie that he could see above the desk, running his tongue between his lips. "I always get what I like."

It was Ronnie's turn to laugh. "Okay, you need to fucking leave. Now."

Mason's face contorted as Ronnie stared at him unaffected. "That dirty mouth of yours could do a lot more than talk." He deliberately took a slow, small step toward her and she knew he was trying to intimidate her. Little did he know, she didn't scare easily.

"You know what your problem is?"

His creepy smile reappeared on his bruising face. "What would that be?" He egged her on.

"It's fairly common. I'm afraid you have little-dick syndrome. It happens to a lot of men. You are overcompensating for your lack of ability to perform. I understand. It's fine. However, this alpha-male stalker complex you have going on isn't going to work in your favor. Not on me."

"I'm going to teach you a better use for that fucking mouth," Mason threatened as his wide eyes turned into slits and his mouth twitched.

Ronnie laughed. "You're not the first person who doesn't like my mouth."

"Oh, I like it just fine."

"Get the fuck out. You're wasting my time."

"I'm not going anywhere." He walked around the desk and stepped behind it, brushing up against Ronnie. She could almost feel a thick coat of slime covering her skin as his bare arm rubbed against hers. Her body stilled, and for the first time since Mason walked through the door, the smallest dab of fear found its way into her mind.

"What the hell is going on?" Mic said, coming down the hall. Ronnie sighed inwardly as Mason stepped back.

"Nothing, just wanted to see what this woman could do for me." Mason stepped away from the reception desk and headed for the door.

"Right. I won't be doing anything for you." The words left Ronnie's mouth in a snarl that made Mic's face contort in confusion.

As Mason gripped the door handle, he turned his head over his shoulder and smiled at Ronnie. The way his lips curled over his teeth made her suddenly nauseous. "Bye, Ronnie." He laughed, and then walked out.

"What the hell was that?" Mic swung his head back around to look at Ronnie, worry molding deep lines around his mouth.

"It was nothing, some asshole that Kale knows—he likes to bark, but he's got the bite of a toothless puppy."

"And who the hell is Kale?"

Ronnie's eyebrows darted toward her hairline, a gesture that seemed to be present in all of her and Mic's conversations today. "He's the guy I tattooed the other night, the soldier."

"Oh," Mic said, drawing out the word as the pieces fit together. "And this soldier is already bringing you drama?"

"No," Ronnie snapped defensively. "We ran into that jackass yesterday. It's nothing," she said. She needed to call Kale to let him know his good old buddy was in town. He would probably be next in line for an oh so pleasant visit, and she wanted to warn him.

The door chimed again, and Ronnie involuntarily held her breath as she turned toward the door, hoping like hell it wasn't Mason again. Luckily, it wasn't.

"Can I help you?" Ronnie asked as two girls walked in.

"Yeah, we have an appointment with Ronnie Clark."

"That's me," she sighed, and sent a silent prayer out to the Tattoo Gods that these girls weren't going to want matching ink. "Come on back."

After her run-in with Mason and a long day of tattooing an unfortunate amount of peoples' asses—tattoos that would more than likely be lasered off in less than a year's time anyway—Ronnie was tired, hungry and ready for bed. But she had told Jordan she would meet her for dinner and a drink and hell, who was she kidding? She never passed up food and liquor.

She tucked her chin and nose down into her wool scarf as she walked from the parking lot to Sidelines Bar and Grill. It was starting to snow, she'd had to park all the way out in Bum-fuck, Egypt, and she feared for the feeling in her nose, and fingertips for that matter. Sidelines was always packed and it was especially busy on Wednesday nights when they had their hump-day deals, dollar domestic longnecks. The bar was more than likely full of soldiers and all other forms of assholes. She would have much rather gone to her little hole-in-the-wall, blacklisted bar full of big biker men and drunk old perverts, but Jordan had picked the place. At least they had good burgers.

When Ronnie opened the door and walked inside she was surrounded with the aroma of pizza and burgers and it instantly made her stomach rumble. The bar was crammed full of people and all the tables were occupied. Ronnie hoped like hell that Jordan already had a table because she was not waiting any longer than she had to.

Just as her head was navigating from one side of the bar making its way to the other, Jordan came into view, blocking her way.

"Come on, let's go," Jordan said when she reached Ronnie.

"What? I just got here, what the hell?"

"Well, I'm in the mood for Mexican and margaritas and

this place is too busy so let's just go." The urgent desperation in Jordan's voice had Ronnie stopping like she was a deadweight of bricks.

She narrowed her eyes and hoisted her hands on her hips. "Jordan, don't bullshit me. What's up?"

"Nothing," Jordan lied; she was a completely horrible liar so Ronnie saw right through it. If Jordan was lying to her then she had a reason, and Ronnie was going to find out what that reason was.

"Get out of the way, Jordy," Ronnie said, pushing past Jordan, moving out of the hostess area and into the bar where all the tables were. She didn't even need to look around for more than a breath. Sitting on the far side of the room was Kale. She would recognize that sandy brown hair, preppy boy, Captain America impersonator in a pitch-black room with night-vision goggles on. It was him, and he was with a woman—a fucking blonde, for crying out loud. Of course, she had to be beautiful as well. Big straight smile, tiny waist, round eyes that were probably blue, and of course she had big boobs that girls paid thousands of dollars for and Ronnie was willing to bet her left tit that they were real. Fucking fantastic. Of course she looked like his type too. Snug-fit jeans and a cream-colored sweater with a long, thin scarf looped on her neck. She was just as model-worthy as he was.

Blondie was sitting frustratingly close to Kale, and she had her hand placed on his chest. She was laughing and he was smiling at her and it was apparent that he was having a good time. They obviously had an intimate relationship together too. Ronnie could tell by the easy way he held himself under her hand, and the way her legs angled toward his body, and the way she leaned into him as she talked.

"Ronnie, let's go," Jordan said, coming up behind her.

It was as if the sound of Ronnie's name coming out of Jordan's mouth physically snapped Kale's head toward her. His smile fell when his eyes locked on Ronnie and he instantly stood up, concern etched in every plane on his face.

He started to walk to her but Ronnie immobilized him with a look that would have killed a sniper. He stopped dead in his tracks, never once moving his stormy blue eyes from her.

"Fucking soldier," she hissed.

Jordan looped her arm through Ronnie's and tugged hard, pulling Ronnie's feet from the spot they had cemented to. "Come on, let's go."

"Yeah. Let's go." She peeled her eyes from the tortured stare that was looking back at her, and turned and walked out.

Kale knew this looked bad. When Meagan had called him this afternoon wanting to have dinner together before he left to go back to Iraq, he should have told her no. He didn't want to have dinner with Meagan, he would have rather been with Ronnie, but Meagan was an old friend. She was a sweet girl and dinner with her was better than sitting in his house alone.

The last thing he wanted to do was hurt Ronnie. When he looked up and saw her staring at him, it was like his world went flat and he was slipping off the edge. He had let her down. She thought he did the one thing that had turned her away from love to begin with. He had to talk to her. He needed her to understand.

Kale turned back toward Meagan who was still sitting at the table and he gave her a weak smile and shrugged. "I'm sorry, Meg. I've got to go."

Meagan stood and smiled up at him, her eyes full of understanding. She planted a kiss on his cheek. "Go get her."

"You're the best, Meg."

"I know, I know."

Kale leaned down and kissed her on the top of her head. "Thanks," he said, setting a fifty-dollar bill down on the table to pay for dinner, and then he turned and headed after Ronnie.

He pulled his phone out of his pocket and dialed her number as he walked to his truck. He was surprised when she answered before the first ring was over. He was fully prepared to leave a countless number of voice mails and venture over into stalker territory, driving past her house and the tattoo shop and anywhere else he thought she might be.

"Kale, don't," she said, before any other words were spoken between them. "You have nothing to explain to me. You did nothing wrong." Her words were surprisingly calm and even.

"Ronnie, she—"

"We're not together, Kale. You're not mine. It was just sex, remember? No fluff, just sex. It's fine." Her words may have said she was fine but her voice said otherwise, and the idea that he truly did hurt her was worse than the thought of her not caring at all. He needed to see her; he needed to clear up this misunderstanding. He needed to make things right between them before he left.

"I'm coming over."

"Like hell you are," she spat. Now there was the Ronnie he knew and he was glad to hear the fire back in her voice. "Look, soldier, it was fun, but I'm done. You are leaving in two days anyway. Let's just end our little arrangement with last night."

"Ronnie—" he tried again, but his words were cut short.

"Be safe," she whispered, and then the line went dead.

ELEVEN

Ronnie was still in the parking lot sitting in Jordan's car when Kale had called. She watched him as he rushed to his truck and got inside. She watched as his face fell when she told him that she was fine, and she watched as his body sagged against the back of his seat when she hung up. It was all too fucking much. She didn't want this drama and she didn't want this feeling, the feeling that she had been betrayed yet again; but she wasn't. Kale didn't do anything wrong. She made the mistake of letting go, of letting last night become something it wasn't. No, Kale wasn't the one in the wrong, she was. He was leaving the day after tomorrow and she would become a girl he slept with on Valentine's Day. Now she hated that fucking holiday even more. She didn't think that was even possible, but boy was she wrong.

Jordan turned in her seat to face Ronnie. "You okay?" Her voice was careful and Ronnie hated it.

"Yeah. Why wouldn't I be okay?"

"Well, hum, let's see. Maybe because you just saw the guy

you were sleeping with on a date with another woman, and maybe because yet another man has screwed you over."

"Point out the fucking obvious, why don't you?" Ronnie pulled a deep breath of freezing cold air into her lungs and folded her arms across her chest.

"I'm fine. Did it suck seeing him on a date with that blonde? Yeah, I would have to be dead inside to say that it didn't piss me off. But he can date, fuck, whatever, whomever he wants. He's not mine, and he was never going to be."

"But did you want him to be?"

Ronnie laughed. "No. He was sexy and entertaining, but he was a pain in my ass and a preppy-boy soldier. Not my type. It was just sex."

Jordan looked at her unconvinced, but she knew better than to push the issue. "All right, well, where to now?"

Ronnie looked back over to where Kale had parked his truck. It was gone. She opened the door and stepped out of Jordan's car. "I'm going home. I will talk to you tomorrow." She shut the door and headed to her car. She was even more exhausted now, and with her appetite suddenly gone, all she wanted to do was to curl up in bed and go to sleep.

Ronnie held her coat closed as she walked to her car. The temperature was dropping and a good inch of snow was sticking to the ground. Her heels didn't do much for warmth in this damn weather and her toes were starting to feel the effects of her shoe addiction. She shuffled faster, the cold snow brushing against the top of her feet as she hurried to her car.

The day had taken an unfortunate turn to shitland and she was completely fucking over it. She dug in her purse for her keys as she got closer to her car, cursing the New York winter as her gloved hands felt around. She finally found her keys in her mess of a purse, and the moment her eyes looked up she startled, her heart having a mini spasm when saw someone standing next to her car, someone that any other night she would have rammed her heel up their ass just for bothering her again, but she wasn't in the mood to add ruining a pair of heels to the list of shit that had made this day suck ass.

"Where's soldier boy?" Mason asked when he noticed Ronnie approaching her car.

"You have got to be fucking kidding me." She held her keys tightly in her hands, prepared to stab him in the eye if he even looked at her the wrong way. "You have got to get over it. So you got your ass kicked, big deal. I'm sure it won't be the last time."

Mason moved away from the car and took quick, deliberate steps toward Ronnie. Something in the way his eyes roamed over her made her steps stall, her instincts going on high alert. Kale's warning about Mason showed up front and center in her mind. Fuck . . . Kale. She never told him that Mason was here. Did he even know?

"What do you want, Mason? This ring-around-the-rosie game is getting a little old. Either tell me what the fuck you want or get the hell out of my way," she said with as much power as she could muster up. With the combination of the cold and the newfound fear that was weaseling its way through her body, it was as good as it was going to get.

Mason stopped directly in front of her, his bulky frame hovering close to her. "Oh, I'm pretty sure you know exactly what I want"—he winked and a chill slithered across Ronnie's skin—"I just want to talk to our friend Kale." He raised his hand, moving it close to Ronnie's head like he was going to run his fingers through her hair and she instinctively pushed his arm away.

"Don't fucking touch me."

"Damn, I like it when you talk dirty." Mason's eyes shifted quickly around the parking lot and then in a movement so quick Ronnie nearly screamed, he had ahold of her arm, his fingers digging into her flesh through the thick material of her coat. He yanked on her arm until her body was pressed flush to him. His body was strong and firm and the width of his chest and arms swallowed her.

Ronnie raised her eyes and looked straight into the ones peering down at her. All the fear had seeped from her the second Mason grabbed ahold of her. The only emotion radiating from her now was pure anger. Her breathing became heavy as she bit her teeth together. "Mason, you have one second to get your fucking hand off of me."

"Or what?"

Ronnie huffed out an annoyed sigh as she brought her knee up, forcefully making contact with Mason's groin at the exact moment she punched him in the chest with her key poking between her fingers. Mason grunted from the impact to his manhood and his hand released her arm as he stumbled back a few steps.

Ronnie quickly pressed the unlock button on her key as she ran the few strides to her car—but she wasn't fast enough.

"You fucking bitch." Mason's hands wrapped around Ronnie's waist, his grip squeezing her skin tightly as he twisted her back around so she was facing him; and then he slammed her against her car, knocking out the little air she had left in her lungs. "You're going to wish you hadn't done that," he said as his rough hand left her waist and wrapped around the back of her neck.

"I'm pretty sure the only thing I'm wishing right now is that I had a knife handy to Lorena Bobbitt your fucking ass. Although, I'm not sure I would be able to find your dick in the first place with it being the size of a toothpick and all."

Mason didn't reply, he just lifted his mouth in that chilling smile, and bit his fingers into the nape of her neck, tangling them with the fine hairs that got caught in his grasp, and she grunted as she tried to jerk away from his hold. Ronnie didn't see the truck pull up; she didn't even hear his shouts when he ran up to them; all she heard was the sound of her heart beating wildly in her ear, and all she could see was red. Ronnie finally snapped back to reality when Mason's body was jerked away from her, some of her hair ripping out as his hand was pulled away.

When her vision cleared, her eyes immediately found Kale—he had Mason on the ground and the snow was beginning to turn red in the space around his head.

"Kale!" Ronnie shouted when her thoughts finally registered the signal to her vocal cords. Her voice was a small distraction, and as his body reacted to the sound, Mason used that little distraction to his advantage, grabbing ahold of Kale's shirt and pulling him down to the ground. In a blink of an eye, Mason was on top of Kale and he got in one good hit, cracking his fist across Kale's face.

Ronnie's breath caught in her chest as the sound of bone meeting bone rang through the silent parking lot. Kale didn't miss a beat, and before she knew it they were both standing again. The look that crossed over Kale's face as he looked into Mason's eyes was raw and frightening. It was like he was a completely different person in that moment. The man who didn't get riled easily was now gone, replaced by a man who was strung out on anger. Kale's body lunged toward Mason, his head lowered and his shoulders hunched over as he moved with the determination of a lineman. Mason's body thundered to the ground, Kale landing punch after punch to Mason's face.

The last thing this night needed was for Kale to be taken to prison for murder, and with the tension rolling through his body, Ronnie was sure he was capable of it.

"Kale, stop!"

Kale's head snapped to hers, every possible emotion creating a pattern of lines that made up his expression—fury smothering the depths of his eyes, guilt twitching in the furrow of his brows, and concern flexing in the angle of his jaw. His chest heaved heavily as he tried to catch his breath. He slowly pushed himself up off the ground and stood facing Ronnie.

She blinked hard, her mind trying to catch up with the string of actions that just happened in the span of a few heartbeats.

Kale's hand released from the fist it was formed into. His knuckles were bleeding and the center of his face was throbbing along with the beat of his heart. He stood there, staring at Ronnie as a look of relief flooded her face. Her body was frozen in place, her expression turning impassive as her eyes softened around the edges.

He looked back to Mason, who was still lying on the snow-covered ground, his coat and face covered in a scarlet sheen. Kale had gone too far, but he didn't care. The feelings that spread through him as he saw Mason's hands on Ronnie were likely to haunt him for the rest of his life.

Kale turned around, his body physically struggling to turn away from the woman who had unknowingly branded him in such a short time. He faced Mason, who was having his own physical struggle trying to get to his feet, as Kale shuffled along the cold pavement toward him.

Kale squatted, lowering his face to him, and Mason flinched as Kale's breath bounced off his battered face. "You will never fucking come near her again, because next time, I won't stop."

He stood up and without looking back, turned and made his way to Ronnie. His steps were quick, his body needing to touch her, to make sure that she was okay.

He didn't stop when he was in front of her; instead he slammed his body to hers and wrapped her tightly in his arms. Her body sagged against him as he held her upright, his arms and chest absorbing her weight as she relaxed into him. Her head molded under his chin and he brushed his lips against her hair, melting the snow that clung to the strands. "Are you okay, Ronnie? God, please tell me you are okay."

"I'm fine, Kale. You swept in and saved the day, I'm fine." She pushed away from him, her hands on his chest. He didn't want to let her go, he didn't want her to push him away, but against every ounce of his being that was aching to keep her pressed safely to him, he let her go.

"Thank you," she whispered. Her eyes shifted to the ground for a brief moment before they returned to his. When he looked back into them, the layers he had worked so hard to peel away were put back in place, shielding any vulnerable emotion she had from him.

"What were you doing back here, anyway?" she asked as she took a small step away from him.

"I never left. After you hung up on me I went and parked over by Meagan's car to make sure she left okay." Kale watched Ronnie's face harden as the words flowed from his frozen lips and he instantly regretted telling her, but he wasn't going to lie. "I'm sorry if I hurt you, Ronnie, but I've never left a woman alone at night, no matter what the circumstance. But I was willing to, to come after you. You know that, right?"

Ronnie swallowed hard, but she didn't say anything. The silence was worse . . .

"After Meagan pulled out, I started to leave and then I saw your car"—the muscles of his jaw moved and tightened underneath his stubble as he worked his teeth together, biting back the image of Mason pressing Ronnie up against her car—"and I saw Mason grab you." He lowered his head and inhaled a deep breath of winter air, trying to smother the heat that was burning his chest.

He lifted his head when he heard Ronnie open her car door. "Ronnie, let me drive you home."

"No, I will be fine. I'm exhausted and all I want to do is

put this night behind me." She paused, her lips pressing together as she looked at him. Then she got in and shut the door without saying another word.

The air blowing out of the vents was barely warmer than the air outside, yet the cool force hitting her face seemed to have a tranquilizing effect. She let it beat against her as she pulled out of the parking lot, driving past Mason as he was struggling to get to his feet. Ronnie smiled. It served that asshole right. The thought crossed her mind to call the cops. Hell, nothing would make her happier than to see his smug, bloody face tucked into the backseat of a squad car, but that would mean getting Kale involved—even more than he already was. She wasn't completely sure, but she assumed beating the shit of out someone in the middle of a parking lot was frowned upon by the Army, and she wasn't going to let Kale get in trouble because of that asshole.

Her tires slipped over the snow as she turned onto the road, her car sliding to the side. Horrible day, followed by a horrible night, and topped off with horrible weather. Fucking fantastic.

Thankfully, her neighborhood wasn't far from the restaurant. The town was small enough to drive from one side to the other in a span of twenty minutes or so, and her neighborhood was smack-dab in the middle. Her car didn't even have a chance to warm up, and her heart didn't even have a chance to slow down, before she was pulling into her driveway.

Ronnie clicked the button on her garage remote and

pulled her car in. She cut the engine and sat there, her body reeling from the whole fucking night. Her hands gripped the steering wheel, her knuckles turning white as she latched on and leaned her head down on her hands. Sure, nothing happened with Mason, nothing serious at least, but her stomach seemed to think otherwise because it was twisting in a knot that not even a Boy Scout could get undone.

And then there was Kale, showing up like the superhero she knew he was. She was surprised he didn't come in with a blue spandex uniform and a giant shield. And when he pulled her in his arms the world seemed to blur around her—and it made him dangerous. He made her feel so many different things all at the same time and it confused the hell out of her. Not even thirty minutes ago she had wanted to scream, or cry, or possibly even both, for the way she felt when she saw him with that blonde, and then when he came back for her, she had never felt happier to see anyone in her entire life. The highs and lows she just went through were equivalent to being in the middle of the ocean, constantly rocking side to side, never feeling still, never feeling grounded. She needed to be grounded; she needed to be in control again.

The darkness behind Ronnie's lids brightened and she lifted her head from her hands to see headlights shining against the back wall of the garage. She didn't need to turn around; she knew exactly who had pulled in behind her.

She pulled the keys from the ignition, opening the door and stepping out in one fluid movement. She leaned her back against her car and waited for him to come to her, knowing he would.

The headlights went out and she heard the truck door shut only seconds before he was in front of her. Kale stood close to her, his chest barely grazing hers, and his head tilted down toward her. He didn't say anything, he just stood there, staring into her eyes with such an intensity that it made tears prick behind them. Nerves fluttered in her chest along with a familiar heartache that she was just finally starting to get over. Kale pulled a deep breath in through his nose and slowly licked his lips. She opened her mouth to tell him to go home but her words were cut off when his hand slid around her waist while the other one intertwined with her hair. He pulled her body to him until there was not one part of her that wasn't touching him, and then his lips crushed hers.

Her mouth stilled, and she froze in place, his large hands holding her from falling against the car as he stunned all the life from her. His lips were unhurried and moved gently over hers with intention. Whether his intention was for his own reassurance or for hers she didn't know, but as his tongue massaged hers, she started not to care.

She sighed, and when the sound reached his ears she felt his firm body that was solid against her soften into her. Her mouth found his rhythm and her lips joined him in the desperate need to feel comfort.

Kale stepped into her and her back pressed into the door of the car, his body leaning over her as he continued to kiss her, his mouth becoming eager and covetous.

His hands left her, but only for a moment. Then they were traveling down her back and around her butt, cupping the flesh above her thighs. He lifted her easily and she wrapped her legs around his waist, her muscles squeezing tightly around him, her body giving in—betraying her.

Somehow in the midst of the raw pleasure she was feeling from Kale's kiss, and from his body molding against her, her mind sent a signal to her heart, and it clenched so tight that she felt a physical pain. She couldn't do this, she couldn't allow herself to be carried away by the comfort she claimed from his body, she couldn't allow herself to hold on to the pleasure she knew would soon follow if she didn't put an end to this.

She dropped her legs, her feet hitting the floor, as she carefully pushed against Kale's chest. She broke their kiss, her lips feeling numb with his absence.

"I'm sorry, Ronnie." He leaned down and brushed his lips over the skin below her ear. "I'm sorry Mason got to you—" he whispered.

"Kale, you have nothing to apologize for. I should have known that he was up to something when he stopped by the shop this morning."

"He came to the shop?" The muscles under his jaw flexed, and his breathing got heavy.

"Yes, I meant to call you to warn you he was in town but I got busy." She brought her hand up to cup his face, to soften the guilt that had hardened his expression, but she hesitated, dropping her hand back to her side.

Kale's face flinched slightly when he felt her reluctance toward him. "I'm sorry you had to see me with Meagan, but—"

"Don't go there right now, Kale. I'm seriously not in the mood to have this conversation right now."

"And when do you want to have this conversation, Ronnie? When I'm halfway around the world?"

She stepped around him. It was hard for her to do because all she wanted was to feel him against her again, but regardless of what she wanted, she knew what she needed. "We don't need to have this conversation at all." She stopped in front of the door that led inside her house and turned around to look at him. He was completely defeated, his eyes tired and miserable, his mouth pulled tight, frustrated. "Go home, Kale," she mumbled softly.

Kale shook his head like each movement to the side was strategically thought out. His legs moved, closing the short distance Ronnie had put between them. He placed his hand over hers that was gripping the door handle, immobilizing her escape from him.

"Why are you doing this, why are you closing me out? You think I don't see in your eyes how you feel about me? You think I don't know how your body responds to mine? I'm calling your bluff, sweetheart."

Ronnie jerked her hand away from his hold and narrowed her eyes at him. "You don't fucking know me, Kale. You think you have me all figured out, huh? You have known me for what, six days? Six days, Kale. You don't have a damn clue how I feel right now."

"You're right, so tell me."

She shook her head as she rolled her eyes and sighed.

He stepped into her, his thick thigh sliding between her legs and sending a trail of goose bumps up her inner thighs. Her body went rigid as he moved his hands to her shoulders, running them down her arms slowly, allowing every nerve in her body to jolt to attention with the soft pressure of his fingertips. His hands stopped at her wrists and held them gently. Ronnie's eyes were glued to Kale's and she watched as he closed his and inhaled sharply. His shoulders leaned forward and his forehead pressed to hers. His eyes remained closed, his blond lashes brushed the top of his cheek, and a slight bruise covered the span of the bridge of his nose, extending under his eyes. She could feel his warm, sweet breath on her mouth, their lips so close to touching that she could almost taste him.

He pulled her wrists up and placed her palms on his chest. He opened his eyes and it seemed as if a fog had lifted around the center. His stare held her prisoner while his body held her captive—all she could do was breathe. "You may not want to talk to me, you may not want to tell me how you feel, but I can feel you"—he pressed her hands against his chest—"in here." Her pulse quickened and she curled her fingers in his shirt. His lips lowered and paused for one breath before he pressed them to hers. His hands still held her wrists and her fingers grabbed onto his shirt like it was her life support as she let go and kissed him back. She savored the taste of his lips, the way his breath felt warm in her mouth, and the way her stomach dropped low, rolling in a sensation that only he was able to give her.

Then he pulled away. His hands released her wrists and her arms dropped to her sides. He leaned forward, placed a chaste kiss to her forehead, and then he turned away from her and left.

TWELVE

Kale woke up the next morning feeling as tired as he had when he went to bed. He hadn't slept worth a shit and he knew it had something to do with a certain snarky woman's body, or lack thereof, lying next to him. Today was his last day in the States until June. Tomorrow he was heading to Syracuse to hop on a plane back to Iraq and he had a couple things he needed to do before he headed back, and talking to Ronnie was his top priority. He knew he'd had to leave her last night, even when it was the last thing he'd wanted to do. She'd needed her space, but he couldn't give her any more. Not today, not when he would be leaving tomorrow. He would run his errands and then swing by the tattoo shop. If he got everything he needed done beforehand then that would leave him more time for her, providing she would give it to him.

"Martin," Kale said as he walked into Bravo Company headquarters. Martin was assigned to rear detachment, taking care of the company's families, facilities, and equipment while the company was deployed.

"Sergeant Emerson, how are you doing?"

"I'm good, Martin. I came to see how things are going here. All the families being taken care of?"

"Yes. I just spoke with the FRG leader this morning to confirm that everything is well."

"What about Fishers's wife? She had her baby the other day. I went to see her in the hospital yesterday and she said she has no family nearby to help her. Make sure that she is set up to have meals brought to her for the next few weeks and child care for her twin boys a few days a week so she can get some rest."

SPC Fishers was one of Kale's young soldiers with a young wife and two-year-old twin boys. The guy got his wife pregnant a few weeks before they deployed and she just had her baby girl a few days ago. Kale promised Fishers that he would personally make sure she was taken care of and that his baby girl was doing well. It was one of the things that was so hard about deployments. His soldier missed the birth of his baby girl, he wouldn't even meet her for four more months, and there was nothing Kale could do about it except take pictures and make sure his wife had the help she needed.

"She was released today and a couple of the FRG members are going to stay with her a few days until she is recovered from her cesarean. I will make sure meals are set up as well."

"Good," Kale said, and he was happy to hear that Martin was already on top of it.

One errand down, one to go.

Kale went to the commissary and loaded his cart full of brownies and Ding Dongs and pretty much every Hostess box of treats that he could find, picked up a couple newly released movies—he was sick to death of watching piss-poor hadji copies that he bought off the Iraqis.

After paying for everything and dropping another hundred and fifty bucks on cigarettes and chew for some of his guys, he headed to the post office to ship the stuff to his company. Then he was going to go to No Regrets to see Ronnie. Hopefully she would want to see him.

"What's with you today?" Mic asked Ronnie as he sat down on the leather couch in the design room.

Ronnie was sitting at the large table sketching in her pad. "Nothing is with me! Why the hell are you riding my ass so much lately? Do I usually look like a ray of fucking sunshine? No."

Yes, Ronnie was in a particularly sour mood today, but she was entitled to one. Yesterday had been a day from hell. She hadn't slept at all. Her mind kept returning to the image of stormy blue eyes looking into hers as they broke piece by piece before he turned and walked away from her. But it's what she wanted, it was for the best. He would be gone tomorrow.

When she woke up this morning, there was a fresh blanket of snow four inches deep on the ground, she was out of coffee, the line at Starbucks was fucking ridiculous, and her first appointment of the day was a no-show. She was having another shitty day to say the least and she wasn't going to pretend like she wasn't.

Mic popped a doughnut into his mouth. It was already one in the afternoon but in Mic time, it was morning. "All right, I was just checking. I would like to keep my head, please, no need to bite it off."

Ronnie kept her eyes focused on her sketch. "Shut up and eat your doughnuts and let me work in peace."

Mic stretched his arms out and then stood up from the couch. "All right, Angel," he said, and then he left Ronnie to herself.

Ronnie had a slow day today. Of course, she would only have two scheduled appointments—although now she was down to one—on the one day she would like to bury herself in hours upon hours of work. Even tattooing hearts and lockets and love on sappy young newlywed Army wives would be better than sitting on her ass thinking about . . . No, she wasn't going to fucking think about it.

"Hey," Harold said, popping his head into the design room. "Your security system company is on the phone. Someone broke into your house."

"What?" Ronnie jumped out of her seat and ran out of the room. She picked the phone up off the reception desk. "This is Ronnie Clark."

"Mrs. Clark, this is Andrea Thompson at First Choice Security—"

"Yes, I know. What's going on?" Ronnie interrupted. She didn't care who she was, she just wanted to know what the hell happened.

"Yes, well, we reported a break-in at your home address through a window on the north side of your house. The police have been notified and they are currently en route to investigate. It is suggested that you wait for the police to contact you."

Mason.

"Thanks." She slammed down the phone onto the receiver. Like hell she was going to wait for the police to contact her.

Ronnie rushed back to the design room and grabbed her purse. "Mic, cancel my appointment today, tell them I will call to reschedule."

"What happened?" he hollered from his room.

"I will let you know when I find out."

She walked out of the door, tramping through the snow to her car. This is the last thing she needed right now. Mason picked the wrong day to mess with her. She had had it up to her eyeballs with his bullshit and breaking into her house was adding a whole new level of pissed-off to Ronnie's temper.

She almost called Kale—but she didn't. The simple fact that he was the very first person that came to her mind was reason enough not to call him. Besides, the cops would be there to handle Mason. She didn't need a superhero to come rescue her, not this time.

Ronnie was surprised to see the cops pulling out of her neighborhood as she was turning in. Why wouldn't they have waited for her, or at least contacted her?

Ronnie took a deep breath before she pulled her car into the driveway. Weirdly enough, considering there was an alleged break-in, nothing seemed out of the ordinary. She opened up the garage door to pull her car in, and her heart instantly wedged its way into her throat. Sitting on the ground next to the door that led into the house was an all-too-familiar pair of combat boots. Fucking fantastic.

Ronnie shut the engine off and sat in her car. Maybe she should just leave, pretend like she never came home. She couldn't deal with this right now; she would have rather found Mason and the cops here. She wasn't prepared for this, and being blindsided was not how she wanted to handle the situation when the situation finally came. However, it didn't look like she had much of a choice because at that very moment, the door opened and Brandon walked into view.

Her heart slipped from its lodged position in her throat to the pit of her stomach when his eyes met hers through the windshield and he offered her that sweet, slight smile of his that she had always loved.

Reluctantly, she opened the car door and stepped out. She just stood there next to her car, staring at the man she thought she would spend the rest of her life with; the man who took her heart and put it through the snowblower, scattering the tiny pieces in every which direction, making it impossible to find them all. It was him. He was standing there in his tan T-shirt and ACU pants looking as good as she remembered. The tattoo on his biceps she gave him a few years ago was peeking out from the sleeve of his shirt. She could see his defined chest through the cotton fabric, his dog tags hanging low on his neck between the muscles. His hair looked freshly buzzed, leaving his dark brown hair tight to his scalp. He looked like her Brandon, only he wasn't her Brandon—not anymore.

"Hi, Ron," he said, her name rolling out of his mouth like it had every day since the day she met him. It sounded the same, it sounded like it had when she was his, when he hadn't fucked up and betrayed her—but it wasn't the same now.

"What are you doing here, Brandon?"

"I've been trying to get ahold of you to tell you I was coming home on leave but you were dodging my calls."

"You think? I didn't want to talk to you. I don't have anything to say."

"I think we have a lot to say. We have a lot we need to talk about."

Ronnie walked toward the door, ice spitting from her cold stare as she shoved Brandon out of her way so she could go inside.

He followed her into the house.

"You're the person who broke into the house?"

"My key didn't work," he said behind her as she walked into the kitchen.

"No shit, I changed the locks."

"When did you get a security system?"

"The week you left for Afghanistan. It was either a security system or a dog, and we both know I'm not an animal person."

"I'm sorry, Ron." His words were soft but she could hear him clearly—he was right behind her. He placed his hand on the small of her back and she spun around so quickly she was surprised she didn't sever his limb.

"You're sorry? Well, it's too fucking late for that."

"Why? Why does it have to be too late? I still love you."

"Don't you dare tell me you love me, Brandon. If you did you wouldn't have cheated on me. You don't get to come home and pull this shit." She yanked off her boots and stormed to her bedroom, hoping to get away from him, but she should have known better. She could hear his heavy footsteps following her until they stopped just inside her bedroom door. She didn't need to turn around to know he was resting his tall, lean, perfectly sculpted body against the door. She didn't need to turn around to know he was watching her carefully like he always did when she was upset.

"Don't do this, Ron. I love you, you know I do."

That was the final blow. She wasn't going to be made out to be the bad guy for ending things. This was all on him.

"Tell me why."

"Ronnie . . ." His voice was quiet, and he at least had the decency to look regretful. He took another step into the room and Ronnie held her hands out in front of her to stop him.

"Just tell me why."

He lowered his head but kept his eyes on her. "I don't have a reason why. It just happened."

Ronnie shook her head and sighed. She wanted the truth. She needed the fucking truth. "I deserve more than that."

"Look, I made a mistake. I had just gotten off a mission. We were in a blackout so all the phones and servers were down. I was missing you like crazy and I was pissed off that I couldn't talk to you."

Ronnie's eyes filled up with unshed tears, making it hard

for her to focus. If she blinked, they would spill over and she was determined not to let him see her cry. Ronnie never cried.

His gray eyes traveled over her face, hoping for something that she couldn't give him. "It just happened."

Ronnie chest heaved as she took in a deep breath, her back shaking as she held in the sob that was trying to break through. She walked to her dresser and pulled out a sweatshirt. Before she even realized what she was doing, she peeled off her shirt, standing in her bra. She had been with him so long that her mind and her body were still comfortable with him, even if her heart wasn't. She paused as she felt the heat of Brandon's stare. She glanced back at him and he was looking at her with desire in his eyes, a look that he no longer was entitled to. She pulled the sweatshirt on over her head and stepped into her furry slipper boots. She marched toward him, not giving him the satisfaction of a look as she walked past him and into the living room.

He was like a lost little puppy dog following her from room to room and she just wanted him to leave.

Brandon stepped in front of her as she sat down on the couch. "Ronnie, will you fucking talk to me, please?"

"What do you want me to say?"

"Anything. Just tell me what is going on inside your head. Please." He sat down next to her on the couch, a little closer than she would have liked, but still far enough away that they couldn't reach each other.

She saw him, the Brandon she has always known and

loved. She saw the guy from the wrong side of the tracks, the bad boy with a big heart and big dreams. He was the guy who saved her from her empty life, the guy who took nothing and made something. He was her Brandon.

Ronnie closed her eyes as she sucked air into her lungs and blew it out through her nose. When she opened her eyes, she turned them to Brandon. "I love you, Brandon." The words were stuck in her throat but she had to get them out. "You came into my life when I needed someone most, when I needed rescuing. And you rescued me. I needed you and you were there. But I don't need you anymore." She was surprised at how calm her voice was, especially since she was screaming inside, the anger and the pain—it was all boiling over inside her.

"You don't need me anymore? Well, that's pretty fucking convenient, Ron. So what? It's over?" Brandon had a short fuse and his temper was starting to flare. Ronnie knew it wouldn't be long before hers joined in. They were both bombs ready to detonate and they each held the trigger for the other. It had always been that way.

"Yes, it's over." Her voice was on the verge of shouting as her patience was wearing thin. "It's been over for months now."

Brandon made a noise that sounded like a growl as he shook his head at her.

"How many times, Brandon?"

"What?" he asked, blinking at her, and she could tell in that moment that he was shuffling through his mind for something to say, and that something was going to be a lie.

"I'm not stupid. How many other times have you cheated on me? Don't even fucking think about lying to me because it won't work."

Brandon looked at her and she could tell he was weighing his options, trying to decide which fate would be the better one, which way out would be the easiest.

"I want the truth. You know I deserve it."

"Just one other woman," he said quickly.

Ronnie pressed her lips tightly together and nodded her head. "One other time or one other woman?"

He didn't answer and he didn't need to. The look in his eyes said it all. "You need to leave," she said, standing up and walking toward the door. He stood up but he didn't make a move to follow her.

"I'm not leaving, Ron."

"Brandon, do you think you would have cheated on me if you truly loved me? Do you think you would have needed another woman if I was it for you? Stop pretending. We fell in love young, we became each other's safety net, and we let ourselves stay there. You don't love me the way you should." She was screaming at him and it felt good. It felt good to let out all the hurt and betrayal that had taken up the space of her heart.

"You're wrong, Ron," he said softly. "I have loved you since I met you. I do love you."

"I know." The calm started to return in her chest but it brought with it a fresh batch of heartbreak. "I know you love me, but not enough. Not the right way."

Ronnie felt the bastard tears re-forming as the back of

her throat started to burn with the need to let those tears fall free. Her chest constricted and she couldn't hold them back any longer. Just as they spilled over her bottom lashes, the doorbell rang. Could this day get any fucking worse?

Apparently so. The Gods seemed to have opened up the skies and a shit storm came pouring down on Ronnie, drenching her from head to toe, because standing on the other side of the door was Kale.

Ronnie's eyes dropped to the ground when she saw the look that crossed over his face when she answered the door. "Now's not a good time, Kale." She didn't want him to see her crying too.

He stepped into her and lifted her chin with his fingers. "What's wrong?" His voice was urgent and determined as he searched her face for the slightest inkling of a reason for her tears.

Ronnie felt Brandon come up behind her, so close that his chest brushed across her back. "Who are you?" Brandon asked as he eyed Kale, and Ronnie knew things were about to get heated. Brandon was protective, and she got the impression that Kale was too.

"I'm Sergeant First Class Emerson. Who are you?" Kale stepped even closer to Ronnie but she softly pushed against him so he would move back. He looked down at her but his face didn't give anything away.

"Sergeant Brandon—"

"You're Brandon?" Kale interrupted, not needing to hear his last name, knowing exactly who Brandon was. "You have got to be kidding me. Ronnie?" He tore his eyes from Brandon who was still hovering behind Ronnie and moved them to her.

A fresh stream of tears streaked down her cheeks. It seemed as though she had opened the fucking floodgate and they wouldn't stop coming. Kale gently grabbed ahold of her arms, looking her hard in the eyes. "Ronnie, are you okay?" He said the words slowly like he was letting each one sink in before moving on to the next.

Ronnie jerked out of his hold and wiped her face with the back of her hand. "I'm fine. What are you doing here?"

"I came to see you. I needed to see you before I left."

"Ronnie, who the fuck is this guy?" Brandon asked, stepping up next to her, his shoulder pressing against hers.

"Brandon," Ronnie warned, sending him a glare from hell as she stepped away from him.

"Can we talk?" Kale asked, bringing her attention back to him.

"Ronnie, you'd better start fucking talking. Who is this guy?" Brandon's teeth were grinding together, his body unmoving next to Ronnie as he stared at Kale.

Kale moved to the side so he was now chest to chest with Brandon. Kale was bigger than Brandon, but they stood nose to nose at the exact same height. "Look man, you may have talked to her like that in the past but you will not talk to her like that again, do you hear me?" Kale's voice was calm but the threat laced in his words was perfectly clear.

Ronnie had reached her limit for the day, hell, she had reached her limit for the fucking year. It was time for a drink and a bath followed by her bed. "Both of you out."

"What?" They both said at the same time.

"Brandon, get out. We are done. We have been done for months now and you know it. Leave. I don't care where you go but you are not staying here. We can talk later about selling the house."

"Ronnie, I'm not—"

"Brandon, please?" Ronnie begged, because she knew that deep down Brandon couldn't deny her something she wanted. He never could, it was his weakness.

Brandon looked at her and nodded. He picked up his duffel bag, which was sitting in the hall, and headed toward the garage. She was surprised at how easily he walked away, that wasn't like him at all, but she wasn't going to question it.

She turned to Kale, her eyes going softer when she looked at him. "Just leave," she whispered.

"I don't—" Kale started but stopped when she looked up at him.

"Go," she said again, her voice slightly stronger than the last time. The tears started spilling again and she wanted to fucking slap herself for being such a whiny little girl. "This is exactly what I didn't want, Kale. I didn't want some man hovering over me like a fucking guard dog. I didn't want you to be here. I didn't want the line to get blurry, and I sure as hell didn't want you to cross it. Our arrangement is over, just go."

He looked at her, unblinking as he inhaled a deep breath and released it slowly. "All right, sweetheart, I'll go." He pulled her in his arms before she realized what he was doing. His strong arms felt good as he held her against him, and she let him. Why are the things that feel so right so completely wrong?

He kissed her forehead. "Bye," he whispered against her skin, and the longing in his voice made the ache in her chest throb.

She stepped back and shut the door, sagging against it, and then everything washed out of her like a colossal tsunami.

THIRTEEN

Small flakes of snow were drifting from the sky, adding a light dusting to the already white ground. It was early, just after eight in the morning, and Kale's flight was scheduled to leave in ten minutes. In ten minutes, he would be back on a plane—the first of several, until he reached his destination—back to his platoon, back to his mission. It's what had always mattered, what had always been his top priority, but it wasn't anymore.

Kale was sitting down waiting to board the plane, staring mindlessly at his iPad, thinking about everything in the last thirty-six hours that went wrong. And now it was too late for him to fix it. The one woman that had ever made him want more didn't want a thing to do with love, or a soldier.

An older woman sat down across from him and pulled what he assumed was her grandson up onto her lap. The kid must have been six or so and he was staring at Kale like he was a giant GI Joe.

"Hey, little buddy," Kale said, finally acknowledging the little guy.

"Are you gonna die?" the little towhead asked like he was asking Kale what his favorite color was.

"Rylan. You can't just say things like that," the woman admonished, looking absolutely mortified.

Kale smiled. Leave it to a kid to ask the toughest question in the easiest way possible. "Nah, I'm not gonna die."

"My friend at school told me that soldiers always die," the kid said. His face was easy, his eyes curious and hopeful.

Kale swallowed hard, his throat choking on the words as they left his mouth. "Well, that's not true. Soldiers don't always die."

"So you're not gonna die?" he asked again, talking about death with a smile on his face.

"Nah, I'm kind of indestructible. You like superheroes?"

The little boy nodded and his grandmother smiled apologetically at Kale. "Well, I'm sort of like Captain America." This time Kale smiled and he couldn't help letting his laugh slip through when the kid threw his arms across his chest and gave him a challenging look of disbelief.

"Then where's your shield?"

"He doesn't need a shield, kid, but he is Captain America. I promise," a sweet voice said from behind Kale, making his body suddenly tense from the pleasant surprise of the sound reaching his ears.

When Kale stood up and turned around, he was shocked to see Ronnie standing there. God, she was beautiful.

"Hey, sweetheart." He walked around the chair and stood in front of her, giving them a little privacy from the rest of the people waiting.

She smiled and it made Kale want to take her right there, just so he could feel her, just so he could taste her one last time.

She shook her head at him. "Hey, soldier. You'd think you would have learned after I told you the first time. You really need to stop mind-fucking me."

Kale laughed. "Sorry, baby, no can do. The image is permanently burned into my mind and I plan on using it to help me get through some lonely nights," he said teasingly. He let his eyes drop to her mouth, to those cherry red lips, and everything left him except for the need to kiss her.

He forced himself to meet her eyes again because looking at lips he so desperately needed to kiss was torture. "What are you doing here, Ronnie?"

"I couldn't let you leave without telling you good-bye. We didn't really end on a good note and I would have hated myself if I'd let you go without saying 'bye."

"You could have called me instead of driving the hour and a half to Syracuse just to tell me 'bye. I mean, don't get me wrong, sweetheart, I'm really glad you did but you didn't need to drive out here with all this snow on the ground and—"

"Kale," she said softly.

He stopped and looked at her. They held each other's eyes, neither one saying anything to the other, neither one needing to at that moment—it was all there encrypted in the flecks that dotted their irises. He saw regret in hers, mirroring back the feeling that was eating a hole in his heart. The only difference was, he wasn't sure her regret matched his own—the regret of not having more, more time, more . . . her. Her eyes lowered, breaking the trance that Kale was under. He watched her chest rise slowly then drop heavily as a dubious sigh left her lungs. When she lifted her gaze back to him, a magnetic force took over his limbs and he reached out, pulled her into his arms, and held her—and she let him. She melted against him and it felt so right that it hurt. It hurt because he was going to have to let her go. Even if by some miracle she wanted him, he was leaving—he had to leave.

But first, he needed to make her understand.

"Hey, about the other night," he said with his face buried into her long hair.

She didn't move, she just continued to let him hold her. "Kale, I said it's fine."

"No, it's not." He pulled back from her so he could look her in the eyes. "Meagan is an old friend. I was with her in the past but it was before I deployed, it was before I met you. She is just a friend, nothing more. Ronnie, it was just a meal. Believe me, I wanted it to be you; I still want it to be you."

She didn't say anything; she just held his eyes stolidly so he continued. "I just couldn't let you think that I was out with another woman—that I was going to sleep with another woman. I don't care about our arrangement. I don't care if it was just sex, I wouldn't do that to you."

She nodded and Kale's body relaxed. "You don't owe me an explanation," she said carefully, her voice cracking slightly.

Kale shook his head and sighed. She still didn't get it. "Our arrangement was the best thing that happened to me," he said, gently curling his fingers around her chin. He needed to see her eyes.

Her brows lifted and she smirked. "Oh really?"

Kale laughed. "Of course because the sex was amazing," he said, knowing exactly what she was implying. "But also because I got to have you." He pushed aside the hair that was draped across her shoulder and it tumbled down her back. He softly ran his knuckles down the side of her neck, splaying his fingers out at the base of her throat, feeling her erotic pulse patter against the thin, delicate flesh above her collar. "I want more. I want all of you, Ronnie. Not just the sex."

"Kale—" she started, but he wouldn't let her finish. He needed her to know how he felt.

"Quit being so stubborn and listen to me," he said sternly, but he couldn't help his lips twitching when the whites of her eyes almost completely disappeared through the slit in her lids.

"You're exasperating, sweetheart. I—" His words were cut off by the flight attendant's voice carrying over the intercom. He looked back and saw people starting to board the plane. This was it. He was leaving.

Without saying another word, he turned back to her and kissed her. He pulled her in his arms, slid a strong hand through her hair, held her tightly to him, and kissed her. It was desperate and it was sexy and it was the single best moment he had had with this woman. His lips caressed hers, her tongue slowly tangling with his. He poured everything he had ever felt for her into that kiss and she gave it right back to him, dripping every ounce of her into him. Her hands wrapped around his waist as she clung to him, and he tasted her tears as they silently dripped down her cheeks and onto their joined lips.

She pulled away all too quickly. He wasn't done savoring what he could of her. She looked up at him and smiled slightly, but all he saw was pain in her beautiful brown eyes.

"Good-bye, Kale," she whispered. Then he watched her walk away.

She could feel her mascara clinging to her cheeks as she walked away from the terminal gate. She could feel a singe in her back from the heat of Kale's stare as he watched her walk away—as she left him.

She pulled her coat closed with her hand and hurried out of the airport. The freezing air mixed with the moist flakes that still drifted from the sky, clung to her hair and her wet eyelashes. She wanted to curse herself as she felt the wind dry the mascara streaks to her cold cheeks. She hated crying, and she hated that she cried in front of Kale, again. But it was as if she had broken down a fucking dam and the waterworks wouldn't stop coming whenever she was around him. He was a picture-perfect reminder of what she didn't want, what she shouldn't want, and what she wanted regardless of it all.

He was so different from her, her world so different from his, but they fit together like lock and key. Two pieces that need each other to work.

She reached her car and slid inside, quickly turning the ignition and blasting the heat. She lowered her visor and popped up the cover on the mirror. Her cheeks flushed from the cold, her eyes red from her tears, her red lipstick smeared across her swollen lips—she was a fucking mess. She wiped her lips with her thumb in attempts to remove the smudges but all it did was give phantom sensations of Kale's lips caressing hers. She sniffled and wiped the wetness away from under her lashes then tried to remove the black streaks that fell from her eyes creating two long lines—evidence of her weakness.

They weren't coming off. "Get a fucking grip," she told herself, before she shut the visor and pulled out of the parking garage.

He said he wanted more. He said he wanted her, all of her. She shook her head, clearing the words from her mind. He was gone. He was leaving and now she could get back to her normal existence. She could write this off as a lesson learned. Fool her once, shame on you. Fool her twice, shame on her—she was a fool to think that their arrangement would actually work. Shame on her—yes, definitely shame on her.

FOURTEEN

"It doesn't matter if I believe him or not," Ronnie said, wiping the ink off Mic's back as she finished up the last part of his tattoo.

"It does, Angel. A man deserves to know if he is forgiven."

"Who are you? Dr. Phil? He knows I forgive him, he didn't do anything wrong for me to forgive anyway. It still doesn't change anything," she said as she rubbed the needle back and forth, as she shaded in the tattoo.

"I don't understand you. Why are you holding back?"

God, he was seriously getting on her fucking nerves. "You have never been with a soldier. Do you know what it feels like to have the person you care about leave you all the time? Do you know what it feels like to wonder what they are doing or where they are or if they are safe? The military is a great life, sure the men are brave and their families are strong but I can't fucking do it again. I stuck through it with Brandon because we started this journey together and because I thought he was it for me, but I'm not going to do it again. I'm not interested in falling in love. I'm not interested in getting my heart broken again." Even though she was pretty sure it already was.

"I blame you, ya know. I should have never let you tell me that I should sleep with him." Ronnie pulled the tattoo gun away and wiped his back with a little more force than necessary.

Mic sucked in a breath and spoke through his teeth. "Eh, you can't stay mad at me forever. You will get over it. But you might not get over him."

"There is nothing to get over," she said, trying hard to convince herself.

"Keep telling yourself that, Angel. Keep telling yourself that."

Almost a month had passed since Kale left and Ronnie had received a few e-mails from him but that was it. She didn't know how he got her e-mail address, but he did. They were always short and sweet, nothing deep or disheartening. He wrote her about his days and about his men, nothing too detailed or too personal. He would ask questions about her days, about the shop, and about her house. He even would tease her and ask her about her yoga classes. But they were all questions that would remain unanswered. She never responded back. There was no point to getting tangled further into this, whatever "this" was. He was gone, and she was selling the house and moving away. A fresh start.

Ronnie was in her room giving a remembrance tattoo to an eighteen-year-old kid who'd just lost his father in Afghanistan. These ones were the hardest to do. It made her think of Kale and how she'd embedded the names of his friends in his back. It made her think about the look in his eyes when he'd indirectly told her about them. Damn it, it made her think about him, and thinking about him was something she was trying hard not to do.

"You got some flowers," Mic said as he entered the doorway to her room and leaned against the frame, his big beer belly sticking out like a woman who was nine months pregnant.

Ronnie's eyes shot up to look at Mic who was holding a small white card in his hands. "More fucking flowers? Send them home with Harold again. I know his wife loves the weekly bouquet of roses. At least all of Brandon's apology flowers are scoring Harold some major brownie points," Ronnie laughed, and she was thankful for the distraction.

"All right," he said as he turned and walked down the hall. "These aren't roses though. Hopefully his wife likes lilies." She could barely hear him as he got farther away from her room. Did he say lilies?

"I'll be back," Ronnie told the guy in the chair and she walked out of the room and into the reception area. Sure as shit, a big bouquet of stargazer lilies mixed with calla lilies was sitting on the front desk. She came up beside Mic and snatched the card out of his hand. "Let me see that." She had a feeling these weren't from Brandon, and fuck, she was right.

Ronnie,

I don't know if you haven't been receiving my e-mails or if you are just choosing to ignore me. But damn it, Ronnie, I miss you. I miss your smart mouth and your bad attitude. I miss your red lips and your sexy-ass legs. I miss you calling me out on my shit and I miss you rolling those beautiful brown eyes of yours. You changed something inside me, something I didn't ever think I would want, or feel—but you did, and now I can't go back. I want the fluff. I want to give you the flowers and the chocolates. I want to take you out to fancy dinners and buy you gifts. I want you to be my Valentine every day, all day. I want to sweep you off your feet and make love to you every night and wake up to you every morning. I want all of you, not just our arrangement, but all of it. I want all of you.

She read the note one more time, then dropped it in the trash and walked back to her room.

Another few weeks went by. The flowers had long since died, and thankfully, because Ronnie was sick to death of looking at them and smelling their disgustingly wonderful, sweet scent. She didn't have the heart to throw them away so they just sat there on the front desk, wilting and shriveling—dying, until Mic eventually threw them out.

She was finally starting to get back to normal, well, as

normal as normal could be for Ronnie. She had sold her house and was closing on April 4, which was only a few days away. She had everything packed up and loaded on Harold's flatbed trailer, ready to be moved to wherever Ronnie's little heart desired. The problem was she didn't know where. She just knew she couldn't stay here. She couldn't stay here and try to move on with her life at the same time. Not with Brandon returning from Afghanistan in a couple months, and not with Kale coming back here either. She may have made amends with Brandon, but that didn't mean that it was going to be easy seeing him around. Even if she wasn't in love with him, the wounds were still too fresh—too deep. And Kale, she didn't have a fucking idea how to handle that one; she just knew that she was weak where he was concerned. If she truly wanted to move on, to put all of this behind her, then she had to leave.

The bad thing about it all was leaving her guys at the shop. Her whole life she'd wanted a family; she knew now it was the reason she had clung to Brandon for all those years, because he was the only family she had. But she was finally realizing she had one here at the tattoo shop with Harold and Mic and even Jordan. Fucking fantastic, now she was turning into one of those sappy females.

Ronnie had finished her last appointment for the day and she was carrying the last of her stuff out to the reception area. Her room was empty. It was like she had never even been there. It was haunting, seeing it bare and sterile. Someone new would come in and take her place. They would fill the walls with their own art, cover the room in small pieces of themselves. They would move on without her; now she just needed to move on without them—without Brandon, without anyone.

"Excuse me?" A raspy female voice said as Ronnie walked into the reception area. Harold had opened the front door to the shop to allow the fresh spring air into the room so she hadn't heard anyone come in.

Ronnie slammed her box down on the front desk and pushed it out of her way so she could see the customer. Her pupils contracted and her brows furrowed. That damn big-boobed blonde was even prettier up close. Fucking hell.

Ronnie rested her hands on her hips. "Can I help you?"

"You're Ronnie, right?"

"Last time I checked."

The blonde sighed and walked farther into the shop, closer to Ronnie. "Thank God. I have been trying to find you all day."

Ronnie's perfectly waxed dark eyebrows reached her hairline. This blonde was the last person Ronnie wanted looking for her. "Okay. What's your name or should I just call you Stalker?"

The blonde seemed slightly irritated but she planted an indifferent smile on her face anyway. "Sorry, I'm Meagan. I'm friends with—"

"Kale, yes, I know."

"Right." This chick was really getting irritated; it seemed as though Kale stroked her soft spot. "Look,"she said, taking a step closer to Ronnie, her eyes intense like a momma bear protecting her cub. "First, I just want to start off by saying that you're a complete idiot."

Ronnie's eyes widened. "Excuse me? Who the hell do you think you are coming in here and running your damn mouth like that?"

"I'm coming in here as Kale's friend. Kale doesn't fall in love. He has never been in a single relationship because he has never allowed himself to be in one. Then he falls in love with you and you go and break his heart. Do you know just how amazing he is?"

The thought that this Meagan chick knew just how amazing Kale was, in the bedroom and otherwise, made Ronnie want to jump over the desk and strangle her. Just knowing that she had been with him, and that she had felt his strong hard body above her, made bile rise in the back of Ronnie's throat.

"I have never met a better man, or a better soldier, than him. Even though we didn't have a real relationship together, he still treated me better than half of the guys I've been with. Don't waste your chance."

Was she for real right now? "Did you just come here to tell me what to do or did you need something?

"No, I didn't come here to tell you what to do. I just thought you should know beforehand."

"Before what?"

"Before I told you that Kale was home."

Kale was home. He was here. Her nerve endings came back to life as the blood rushed through her veins. "He's here?" she asked, just to make sure she heard her right.

Meagan's eyes shifted to her feet for a brief moment before she raised them back to meet Ronnie's, and in that small amount of time, Ronnie knew—she knew it wasn't good.

"He's hurt." Meagan said the words strongly, like her strength would somehow make it better, but it didn't.

At that very moment, Ronnie's world caved under her feet and she had to brace her hands on the edge of the desk to keep from crumpling to the ground. Her worst fear just materialized out of her nightmares and into reality. From the first night Brandon left for Afghanistan, she dreamed of him getting hurt, of losing him, of death taking him, of never seeing him again. It was always her greatest fear. Since the day she said good-bye to Kale in Syracuse, his image was the center of every good dream and the new focus of all her nightmares.

Her throat constricted, making it almost impossible for her to swallow. Her pulse was racing, and small beads of sweat formed at the back of her neck. "What happened? Is he okay?"

"He's okay now—"

"What happened?" Ronnie asked impatiently. She needed to know, she needed to know how bad he was.

"His Humvee was hit by a roadside bomb. He had shrapnel in his face and thigh. It was pretty bad. They had to perform surgery to remove it and repair some ligaments in his leg. He got back to the States almost a week ago."

"He's been back a week? How do you know all this?" Ronnie asked, sounding like a jealous girlfriend but she didn't give a shit. And if she was honest with herself, she was jealous. Jealous that Meagan has seen him.

"He called me. He needed someone to pick him up from the airport. Believe me, I was his second choice, but since you have been blowing him off he assumed you wanted nothing to do with him, but he's missing you—he needs *you*."

"Where is he now?" Ronnie asked as she grabbed her purse out of the box of her stuff that was still sitting on the desk.

Meagan started toward the door. "He's at his house. Come on, I'll drive you."

"Look, I appreciate you coming here, and telling me, and being the bigger woman and whatnot, but I'm not ready to jump in the car with you and wear friendship bracelets. I'll follow you." Ronnie walked out the door and headed toward her car, Meagan keeping pace next to her.

She laughed. "I can see why he likes you."

Ronnie turned her head and looked at the woman who cared enough about Kale to come and find her. Fuck, now Ronnie kind of had to like her. Damn it. "I just need to make a quick stop first."

FIFTEEN

Kale was sitting at home in his living room and the quiet was almost agonizing. The TV was playing in the background, his iPod was set to shuffle, and the box fan he brought in from his bedroom was running. Yet, it was quiet. The sounds were drowned out like he had hit the mute button in his ears. Instead, it was as if he was watching a silent film in his mind. All he saw was everything caving in around him, everything happening in one single, momentary instant. Then black.

He remembered the few seconds before the explosion. He was talking with the medic that was riding along with them. Kale really liked the guy. He was young—maybe twenty-two. He had a fire to him that Kale respected, a fire that put his whole heart into his job, a fire that reminded Kale of himself. He was a damn good soldier.

They weren't talking about anything in particular, but he remembered the smile on his soldier's face as he retold stories about his daughter—stories they all had heard a hundred times over. He liked hearing his soldiers' stories though, listening about their families. It gave them something to look forward to, something to smile about; and in the hellhole they were in, that was invaluable.

But just as easily as they were talking, just as easily as they were driving down a road they had patrolled time and time again, everything changed.

He didn't remember a sound. He didn't remember the roar of the explosion as it rang through the vehicle, he didn't remember hearing the shouting from his men or the pop of firing weapons. There was only silence.

A singeing pain was ripping apart the skin on his cheek. Hot liquid streamed down his neck, soaking the material of his uniform. His head felt like it was a solid, heavy block of ice. It was a burning pain, but not like a burn from a fire. It was the kind of burn that stung every nerve ending—a cold that burned deep, a cold that was so cold, it hurt.

A fog had lifted in front of his vision, his right eye seeing only a thick haze of gray. He closed his right eye, leaving his left open, and watched as a few of his men went into action, securing the vehicle, tending to those who were severely injured. His young soldier, the medic who had talked about his family only minutes before, was next to him; his head was rolled back and his eyes were closed. His arm was lying across his body like it didn't belong to him, blood covering every visible inch of him. This wasn't the first time Kale's vehicle was hit by a roadside bomb. IEDs happened nearly every damn day and he has been around more than his fair share. Kale knew what he needed to do.

He placed his hands under him and pushed up onto his

feet, but he didn't get far. A strong hand clamped down on his biceps, supporting him as a slicing pain shredded apart his thigh, his body weight crumbling the muscles until it felt like there was nothing left of his leg. The pain traveled up his thigh, through his abdomen, and to his neck. He looked down at his leg as the pain ricocheted to his head. Then his body fell to the floor and everything went black.

The pain meds his doctor prescribed him took the edge off the pain in his thigh but it didn't do a damn thing to dull his mind. He would love to dive into a drunken pity party of liquor until the images were erased from his memory but that wasn't his style. No matter how fucked-up things were right now, he wouldn't go to that place.

He was here. He made it out alive. He wished like hell he could say that about all of them, but they weren't all so lucky.

Tomorrow. Tomorrow he would see them. Tomorrow he would face the little girl who no longer had a daddy. The little girl who would never run into her daddy's arms again, the little girl who would never have the chance to give him hell as a teenager, or have him there to walk her down the aisle when she got married. Kale would have to give his condolences to a young widow who was too young to bear the loss of a husband. Tomorrow. Tomorrow he would relive this hell for them and tell them the stories he was told—he would make sure they knew the last thing their fallen soldier was thinking about was them.

The time after Kale lost consciousness was a complete void. He would slip in and out, and as romance movie clichéd as it was, the one thing Kale thought about when his mind was in working order was Ronnie. When he woke up in Landstuhl Medical Center in Germany, his thoughts instantly went to her; that's when he sent her the flowers. He knew he needed to lay it all out there. He had a second chance and he wasn't going to waste it. But he never heard anything from her. He checked his e-mail every single hour; even if it made him a pathetic sap, he didn't care. But there was nothing, and that was answer enough for him.

When he found out he was coming home, he almost called her. He wanted to see her the second that plane landed on U.S. soil. He needed to see her, but he didn't want her to see him like this. No, if he was going to try to win this woman over, having her pick him up from the airport with a mangled face and a battered leg was not the way to go about it. It had been almost a week now, and the need to see her was getting worse, just adding to the pain that was consuming the rest of his body.

Kale shifted his weight on the couch. He definitely could use one of those old-man LaZBoy recliners right about now. His leather sectional wasn't particularly conducive to the comfort of leg injuries. He leaned his head back against the cold leather and shut his eyes just as a knock on the door broke through the room.

"Come on in!" he shouted.

He heard the door open, then shut, then the soft click of . . . heels? His pulse started to race as a swarm of bees inhabited his chest. He knew the sound of those heels—he knew whom those heels belonged to.

He listened as they clicked down the hall, stopping for a

couple heartbeats before they took the last step, bringing her to the living room, finally bringing her into view.

Ronnie froze, her body going rigid as she stared at him. He couldn't believe she was standing in his living room. She looked more beautiful than he had ever seen her. A tight gray dress clung to her curves and showcased those beautiful legs of hers along with the tattoo that was on her thigh. He smiled when he looked down and saw the bright yellow heels that were on her feet. He took his time scanning back up her body, his eyes landing on her hair that fell around her shoulders in long waves, then to her red lips, which were turned down in a frown. Finally, he moved his gaze to her eyes. She blinked slowly as they collided with his. She set a bouquet of flowers down on the bookshelf next to the hallway and started walking toward him.

Kale pushed himself up with his hands, supporting all his weight on one leg as he reached for his crutches.

"No, sit," she demanded. Her voice was just as sweet as he remembered it.

Kale did as she said, lowering his body back to the couch, wincing as a dull pain shot up through his thigh. "Ronnie, I'm so glad—"

"Don't you dare," she said, stopping just a stride away from him. She was close enough that he could smell her sweet scent, but still too far away for him to reach out and grab onto her.

"I can't fucking believe you." She slammed her palms onto her hips and her thick black brows dipped.

"Ronnie—" Kale tried again, but she cut him short once more, her anger teetering over the surface.

"Why the hell didn't you tell me you were hurt?" she shouted, her voice cracked, and she swallowed hard pressing her lips together as she closed her eyes and inhaled a breath. "Why didn't you tell me you were back?" She opened her eyes and they focused in on the deep gash that ran from the corner of his right eye down to his jaw. It was deep and thick, and the scarring was already evident. He knew it was hideous, he knew his face was never going to look the same again, and he knew his eye would never be back to normal, but when Ronnie looked at him, he somehow didn't feel like a monster.

Her eyes dropped to the floor, and he saw a single tear trickle down her cheek.

"Damn it, sweetheart. Don't cry. I'm fine." He attempted to stand up again but he stopped when Ronnie lifted her gaze and pinned him with a look that paralyzed him.

"I am so fucking mad at you right now."

"I'm sorry," he said. She was mad, but mad at what? That he was hurt, that he didn't tell her he was hurt? He hadn't heard from her and now she was standing in front of him like she was out for blood and he had no idea why. But he was sorry. He was sorry for the tears streaming down her beautiful face, and he was sorry for the pain in her eyes, and he was sorry that he was the one who caused them.

"I feel like I can't even breathe. I feel like . . ." Her words dropped off and she closed her eyes. It felt like a million heartbeats thudded in his chest before she lifted them. She silently crossed the space between them. His eyes grew wide as she climbed onto his lap, straddling his waist. Her hands grabbed the sides of his face and in one swift movement her lips crushed against his, shocking all the air from his lungs. Her lips were soft and sweet, her tears mixing in with the taste of her mouth.

The pain in his thigh she caused as she sat on top of him was worth the reward of feeling her body pressing against him. His body craved this; it craved her like he was a junkie coming off a high. He needed her; he needed to feel her—now more than ever. Kale's hands wound around her waist and he clung to her as if she was going to vanish before his very eyes. He wasn't sure that she wouldn't—this seemed too good to be real.

"I've missed you," he whispered against her lips as he continued to kiss her. A sob caught in the back of her throat and she pressed against him harder, her hands gripping the fabric of his T-shirt. She was kissing him like he was a dying man, and if he was, what a way to go.

The words sliced through her, stinging her insides and warming them at the same time. Who was she kidding, she missed him too. She wouldn't be here right now if she didn't. He inhabited the little space in her heart that was still open—it was small, but he crammed himself into it regardless, and as much as she tried to deny it, to ignore it, she couldn't anymore.

Kale's mouth was so eager, his breathy pants coming in short warm puffs into her mouth. His breath was hot, and he tasted so good. Just like she remembered.

He threaded his fingers through her hair and gently pulled until her lips were no longer on his and her eyes were level with the stormy ones in front of her.

His stare was dangerous. It sucked her in, making her feel like she was spiraling through a black hole that led to somewhere she had never been before. But as scary as it was, it was tantalizing. She would stand on the edge and free-fall down that black hole if it meant being here with him now.

She shifted her eyes to the side of his face where a thick, angry, red scar raised off his cheek in an uneven bumpy line that traveled the length from his eye to his jaw. Ronnie lightly placed the tip of her finger below his eye, on top of his scar. Kale's jaw clinched tight and he shut his eyes as her finger followed the course it took down the side of his face.

Her chest squeezed tight, her heart throbbing in an ache that was so unfamiliar to her she gasped for air. Her throat burned, and she felt a physical pain creep over her body as a sob raked through her back. She held it in, swallowing the anger and the fear that formed her unshed tears.

"You okay?" Kale asked gently. His strong arms locked behind her back and he pulled her close to him so her chest was lying on his. "I'm fine," he whispered in her ear when her face found its way to the dip in his shoulder, her forehead pressed against his jaw, right below his scar.

"It could have been different. You could have—"

"I didn't though. I'm here. I'm fine," he said, kissing the top of her head.

"How the hell can you say that? You can't even walk, and your face . . . your eye—"

"Because you're here. I'm fine because you're here now."

Yes, she was here now, and she needed to reassure herself that he was fine just as much as she wanted to make him feel fine. She tilted her head up and brushed her lips over his jawline. She pressed her palms against his chest and pushed herself up, raining featherlight kisses along the tender ridge that extended down his cheek. His body tensed as she shifted her weight on his lap and she realized she was leaning on his bad leg.

"Damn it, Kale. I'm sorry." She rose up off his lap and started to swing her leg over him to climb off but his fingers bit into the flesh between her hips and her thighs and he pulled her back down on him.

"I don't have a problem with pain, baby," he said, repeating his words from the first time they slept together. A smile tugged on her lips as the memory hit her.

She carefully sank back down on top of him, trying to keep as much of her weight off his leg as possible. "I can see that."

He tightened his hold on her body and pushed her down on him until she was completely on his lap. "I mean it. I want to feel your body on mine, so don't even think about getting up." That impish gleam appeared in his blue eyes, making her smile, annoyingly making her heart do a little pitter-patter in her chest. "I wasn't sure if I would ever get the chance to feel you again; I'm not going to waste it now because of my damn leg."

Ronnie rolled her eyes.

"It's true, sweetheart. I thought about you every day. I thought about being buried deep inside your sweet body . . ."

Ronnie huffed and slapped him in the chest with the back of her hand.

Kale laughed. "Oh, don't think I didn't"—his lips fell from their lopsided grin and his eyes glazed over—"but I also thought about ways to make you mine. I needed you to be mine."

"Kale, I told you how I felt, I told you what I wanted."

"I know, baby. It's what I wanted too—until I had you, but then I needed more. You don't get it. I've never had a relationship with a woman before. I've never wanted one. I've never found anyone that made me want one, till I met you. It was never worth it until you."

"Kale—"

He placed his fingers on her lips to stop her, but the look in his eyes alone sucked the words from her vocal cords. "Don't. Just let me have you this one last night." His hand hooked around the back of her neck and he pulled her down to his mouth before she had a chance to say anything—not that she could have anyway. He was so gentle when he kissed her, his lips just barely grazing hers. She shuddered against him when his hands slid up her leg, traveling agonizingly slowly from her knee up her thigh. His fingers toyed with the hem of her dress, igniting goose bumps on her skin, teasing her as he slipped his fingertips under the edge.

She squirmed on his lap. It had been nearly two months since she had been with him, and the easy way his hands touched her had her quickly slickening between her legs. A raspy moan vibrated in her throat and ricocheted out of her mouth. The sounds caused Kale's fingers to dig into the flesh of her thighs—it was almost painful, but she apparently didn't mind pain either because she fucking liked it. She liked the way he responded to her.

His hands journeyed under her dress and slipped onto her hips. His head jerked away from her so abruptly that she laughed.

"What the hell is this?" His perfectly crafted mouth pulled up in a felicitous grin, his eyes looking at her like she was a shiny new toy on Christmas morning. "No panties?"

Ronnie bit the corner of her lower lip, trying hard not to combust from the look he was giving her. "Do you see how tight this dress is? No panty lines on this girl," she said, intentionally shifting her hips on his lap so she was pressed against him just right . . .

"Damn, sweetheart," he said, sliding her dress up over her hips and latching onto her ass. "I'm one lucky son of a bitch."

His lips slammed against hers, consuming her and possessing her. His tongue parted her lips, tangling with hers, and exploring every last space of her mouth. She needed this too; she needed it just as much as he did. She didn't realize how badly until now. She wanted him to possess her; she wanted him to claim her, to take her for everything she had to offer . . . and more.

"God, I've missed you," he said as he brushed her hair away from her shoulder and pressed his lips to the curve near her neck. "I can't even begin to tell you how much I've missed you. I thought about touching you, tasting you, every day." His lips scattered openmouthed kisses along her collarbone and up the center of her throat, causing her chin to tip toward the ceiling so he could kiss her more. His hands slid up the back of her dress as his teeth nipped at her chin.

"I've missed you too," she admitted, whispering so quietly that she wasn't sure he heard her; she wasn't sure she wanted him to hear her. But he did.

He pulled away, his stormy blue eyes, clouded by desire, quickly cleared as he studied her face. "You did?"

She wanted to laugh, or to fucking punch him in the arm, or maybe even cry at the desperation in his words. The longing they held. It was her fault. She had let him believe that she didn't want more; that she didn't want him. She was so worried about protecting her heart that she forgot to protect his. She was so busy denying it, trying to convince herself that he was nothing more than sex. But she knew better, deep down she knew—and damn it, it hurt.

"Talk to me, baby." His hand left her back and closed around her wrist, gently pulling her hand off his chest. Her eyes followed his hand as he brought her knuckles to his mouth, brushing his lips across them before he kissed each finger. His tenderness plugged her throat, trapping any words she had hoped to say. The way he regarded her was almost terrifying. Not even Brandon had this effect on her. He had never rendered her speechless and motionless by the touch of his lips or the heat of his gaze. No, it wasn't almost terrifying. It was way past that.

"Ronnie"—Kale's hand wrapped around her neck, his thumb massaging the skin below her ear—"are you okay?" His lips brushed across hers briefly before he focused his eyes on her again, trying to coat her with his reassurance.

She distracted herself by pulling up the hem of his T-shirt and lifting it above his head. His surprised expression tugged at her newly sappy heartstrings.

She skimmed her nails up his bare stomach and over his hard chest. A tremble waved through him as she flicked her tongue out and licked the skin above the soft patch of hair on his chest.

"I could have missed this chance"—she lifted her head off his chest and held his gaze with her own vulnerable stare—"I could have missed the chance to tell you . . . to be with you again." Moisture accumulated above her bottom lashes, her throat stinging. What the fuck was wrong with her? Well, she kind of had an idea what it could be. . . .

Ronnie was on an emotional roller coaster—in the last few minutes she had been up and down and around again. It was fucking exhausting.

"But you didn't," Kale said, bringing her back from inside her head. "I'm here."

Yes, he was here, and she wasn't waiting any longer. She climbed off his lap, watching as Kale's eyes followed her every move. She stood between his thighs and pulled her dress off over her head, then reached behind her back and unhooked her bra, letting it drop to the ground.

"You're so beautiful," Kale sighed, drinking in the sight of her naked body in front of him.

She leaned over him, hooked her fingers under the waste of his shorts, and pulled them down along with his boxers, his erection springing free. She pulled them down around his ankles and he lifted his feet so she could pull them completely off. She rose back up, still standing between his massive thighs, and when she looked back down at him, her heart slammed so hard against her lungs she had to force a sharp intake of air into them in order to breathe.

Kale followed her gaze down to his mangled leg. "I know . . ." he sighed.

She met his eyes briefly, her chest heaving with the need to calm down so she could breathe properly. His thigh looked like it had gone through a meat grinder. She thought the side of his face was bad, but nothing compared. She couldn't imagine the pain he felt—it physically hurt her just to look at it. She didn't know how his leg survived such an injury, how he survived.

She didn't know what to say, so she didn't say anything, she just kneeled between his legs. His face went stoic, watching her carefully.

She slid her hands gently up his calves and up to his knees. When she reached the start of his thighs, she met his eyes. His breathing was ragged, his jaw was flexed, his body still, but his eyes—they were easy, soft, and a little bit sad. She slowly and carefully trailed her left hand up his thigh, her fingertips brushing over the tangles of hills and valleys of tissue that rose up off his skin, his leg muscles flexing beneath her touch. She trailed her right hand down his inner thigh until her nails skimmed over the smooth skin at the base of his shaft. His head rolled back and rested against the back of the couch.

She leaned her head forward, fighting back the tears that threatened to form as she looked down at the evidence—at the ugly truth of what he went through. She pressed her lips to the base of the scars that had already started forming on his healing flesh. She dotted kisses up over the ridges and mounds of angry skin, each dusting of her lips causing Kale's body to relax, softening beneath her touch. A wetness she was unaware of streamed hot down her cheeks and splashed in tiny puddles on Kale's leg.

"Baby," he whispered. The tremor in his voice had her stomach momentarily flopping over.

She lifted her head, her eyes absorbing his intense gaze. "I'm so sorry," she whimpered. The sound was so foreign to her, the commiseration in her voice startling her. She hated that this happened to him. She wanted to kiss away his pain, kiss away this horrible nightmare.

"Don't be." His hand cupped the side of her face, his thumb rubbing patterns over her lips. "I'm not." His thumb moved over her cheek, swiping at the tears as they fell.

Ronnie stood. She stood in front of Kale, completely exposed in front of him, never feeling more beautiful in her life. He leaned forward on the couch, quietly grunting as he put pressure on his leg. His large hands clung to her waist and he pulled her closer, her knees hitting the top of the warm leather couch. His fingers traced the tattoo on her hip as his other hand slipped between her legs, his finger testing her dampness. A deep, low moan rumbled in his chest as he plunged another finger inside her heated depths. Her head fell back and she wasn't sure her legs could support her. Just when she thought her knees where going to give out on her, Kale wrapped his arm around her waist, holding her firm, holding her in place as he twisted his fingers inside her, hitting that spot, making her insides clamp down hard on his long fingers. And just like that, just as she was ready to explode, he withdrew from her.

He smiled through his eyes, knowing exactly what he had just done to her. "Come here," he said softly, pulling her down on his lap. "I want to feel you come around me." His erection flicked over her clit and she just about came undone right then. She wanted to feel that too. She wanted to feel him buried deep inside her until she could no longer think straight. She couldn't wait any longer. She lifted her hips, his length springing underneath her, the tip hitting her entrance. She felt a warm drop of his arousal touch her as she slowly started to lower her hips.

Kale's hands grabbed ahold of her, stopping her descent. "Wait. We need a condom."

She leaned her forehead against his, her body trembling with the need to feel him fill her. "It's okay. I'm on the pill." Her voice was shaky.

"Are you sure?" he asked, but his grip on her loosened.

She nodded and sank onto him, slowly allowing her body to stretch to accommodate him. He sighed and he fell backward, pressing into the back of the couch.

"Damn, baby. You feel so good," he said, as she pressed down harder, angling her hips to hit just the right way.

Ronnie leaned down on his chest, her breasts pressing into the spatter of hair that curled between the muscles. He felt good too—better than good. So warm, so. . . . here.

His hands held her face and he kissed her. The feel of his

lips ignited a fire that flowed through her body, straight to her core. She rolled her hips, allowing his length to ease out of her slowly. She was careful not to rest her weight on his bad leg as she rocked her body back and forth.

Kale hung on to Ronnie as her body seeped onto him, swallowing him in her warm depths. Thirty minutes ago, he was trapped in his own head, engulfed in the silence that stretched around him, but now he was so consumed with this confusing woman; and he was grateful for the distraction—more than that, he was just grateful for her.

He could feel the wanton desire dripping from her, adding a thin layer of silk between her thighs, encasing him in her sweet honey. God, she was perfect. He never knew it could feel like this—and he wasn't referring to the sex.

The scar along his face was pulsing along to the rapid beat of his heart and his leg was screaming out in an excruciating pain, but neither one made a dent in the way his body felt having this woman on top of him again. Her body clenched around him, squeezing him tightly as she rolled her hips down, pressing him deep inside her.

Her lips were soft and sweet as she kissed him. He wanted to feel her come undone around him, and he would, but right now all he wanted was to flip her beneath him—he wanted it so damn bad. He wanted to cover her thin body with his and press her into the leather of the couch. He wanted his mouth on hers, everywhere. He wanted to taste her, smell her, kiss her. He wanted to, his leg be damned.

He lifted her off him, her face screwing tightly as his erection left her body.

"What are you doing?" she asked, her voice breathy and coarse as he laid her next to him on the couch.

"I'm trying to get my fill of you," he said as he bit his teeth together and slowly but surely repositioned himself over her. "Although, I'm not sure that is entirely possible." He knew it wasn't. He would never have enough of her. But if this was the last time he had with her, he was going to make sure she remembered it.

His lips found hers again and he kissed her like he was a starving man, which wasn't too far from the truth. He had never felt hungrier in his life, hungry for her. He brushed his lips over her mouth once more before he led the way down her body, taking his time with her breasts, swirling his tongue around her budded nipples. When he was satisfied with the attention he gave to them, he continued down her body, dotting warm kisses along the way. His lips traced over the tender skin above her pubic bone, her stomach trembling from the sensation.

"Kale—" she pleaded, and he loved the way her voice sounded when she begged for him. He would keep her begging for him all night long if he didn't need her so badly himself.

"I know, baby, I know."

He lowered his head, placing his mouth on her soft folds, breathing in, trying to memorize her sweet scent. She was so wet, dripping with arousal. He slowly and deliberately swiped his tongue from the base of her opening to her clit. She bucked and trembled and arched her back off the couch and he splayed his hand out over her stomach to keep her still.

She tasted so sweet, he wanted to savor every lick—he had to. Slowly, he circled her clit with his tongue, tracing over all the other spots he knew would make her squirm. Her legs dropped to the side and he couldn't help the urge he had to dig his fingers into the soft flesh between her ass and her thighs. She moaned and pushed against his mouth, and he adjusted his speed to keep up with her circling hips.

He felt her body quickening, her breaths coming in short quick pants, her hands raking though his hair. He smiled against her glistening opening and plunged his tongue inside.

"Oh . . . Kale . . . please . . ."

He withdrew his tongue, replacing it with his fingers, and licked a path back up to her clit. He stayed there, licking, sucking, and blowing softly while his fingers found her spot, stroking it over and over . . .

Her internal muscles tightened around his fingers as her climax rippled through her, soft moans turning into breathy cries. He rode it out with her, slowing his fingers as the after-shocks contracted around him.

"Kale, please . . ." she whispered, and he knew exactly what she needed, because he needed it too.

SIXTEEN

Ronnie could tell Kale was struggling to lift his body back over her. She could see the vein in his neck bulge as his teeth crushed together—his biceps pulling all of his weight as pain radiated throughout his body. But she could also see the determination in his eyes. He was going to have her this way even if it killed him—she just hoped it wouldn't.

When his heavy body finally covered her, she wanted to fucking sigh at the elation that she felt coursing through her veins.

He smiled down at her, his dimple drilling deeply into his scruffy cheek. "Hey, baby."

Ronnie couldn't resist an eye roll. "Hey, yourself. Took you long enough," she teased, trying to lighten the situation that had crept between them as he was struggling.

"Yeah, sorry about that." He winked and then lowered his hips until she felt his length press against her sensitive entrance. She pulled her knees up, opening up for him, practically begging for him to enter her.

But instead, he lifted his hips so she could no longer feel him against her there. Her bottom lip involuntarily stuck out in a pout as the cool air stung her in his absence. Kale leaned down, grazing his teeth over her bottom lip. "I can take longer if you like, make you wait it out a little—"

"No!"

Kale just laughed and dove into her. In one swift thrust, he was inside her and all felt right again.

Ronnie lifted her arms, locking them through his arms and around his shoulders, pressing him to her. "Thank you," she said, smirking.

"Anytime, sweetheart."

Kale's blue eyes held hers and she watched as the playfulness that wrapped around them faded. Fuck. She didn't want it to fade; she didn't think she could handle another whiplash of emotions thrown at her. The last thirty minutes or so were enough. Now she just wanted to get lost in him.

"Hey," she said, grabbing his face between her hands, careful not to put pressure on his right cheek. "No more serious stuff, okay? Let's just enjoy each other."

His forehead dropped to her shoulder, his hands on each side of her head, supporting his weight. "I can't do that," he said into the curve of her neck.

"What?"

Kale lifted his head, his eyes sweeping to hers. "Any other time—any other woman, and I would have gladly put the serious stuff away and fucked you till I couldn't see straight, but you're not some other woman." Ronnie didn't say anything. What could she say?

She tightened her muscles around his hard length, which was unmoving inside her, and wiggled her hips. She wanted him—she needed him. "Please, Kale . . ." she said, circling her hips again.

A growl rumbled in his chest and she could physically see his resolve faltering. He slowly, too slowly, pulled his hips back. Just as the last inch of him was about to leave her, he plunged back into her, knocking the air from her chest. He stayed there, rolling his hips, swirling around deep inside her. She was already so sensitive, and every little move he made had her tingling from the inside out.

His mouth found its way to hers again. He kissed her softly, his tongue barely dipping into her warm mouth. He paid attention to her bottom lip, pulling it gently with his teeth, sweeping his tongue across it. He was tender. His hands, his mouth, his body—he definitely hadn't put the serious stuff aside, and now Ronnie was glad. Feeling him like this was . . . healing.

"You have ruined me, sweetheart," he said, brushing his thumb over the thin skin at the base of her throat.

His words crumbled around her at the same time they built her up and held her high. Having that power over him was scary, yes, but she would be lying to herself if she said that she didn't like it. Knowing that he felt so strongly for her that he yielded the power of his happiness over to her, that she was the one capable of making or breaking him—it was what she wanted. Isn't that what most everyone wants? To be loved by someone so fiercely that you hold their world in your hands, that you are the one to keep it safe. It was fucking terrifying.

But she didn't want to ruin him. Not at all.

Kale's mouth moved to her neck, right below her ear, and all thoughts washed away from her clouded mind. All she could think about now was the way his body felt above hers, they way his mouth heated her skin, and the way his scent encased her. She was lost; she was finally lost in him.

"It could be like this every day, you know. I could do that to you every single day," Kale said when he finally rolled off Ronnie, pulling her against his chest. He was spent, and he could tell that she was as well. Her body trembled, shaking from the intense aftershocks of her orgasm. She had come around him so hard, her body squeezing every bit of him as he pumped into her. And he had savored every last bit of it.

He didn't want to roll off her. He didn't want to leave her body, leave the warmth that clung to him—but he had to. With the feeling of this woman no longer squirming beneath him, his screaming leg took up the space of sensation that she previously inhabited.

One of Ronnie's dark brows lifted. "Cocky much?"

"Baby, I don't need to be cocky, I'm just telling you how it is."

"Uh-huh, okay." She rolled her eyes and snuggled into his chest. He was a little surprised that she was still in his arms, that she was allowing him to hold her. But he would take her anyway he could get her, no way in hell was he complaining. He would hold her until morning if she would let him.

"It could though, sweetheart. It's not all that bad."

Her mouth breathed warm breath on his shoulder when she spoke. "How would you know? You've never been in a relationship."

"You got me there. But if being in a relationship means that I get to feel this every day"—he placed his hand on her side and ran it down the length of her body, then pulled her hand up and placed it over his chest, over his heart—"and feel this every day, then sign me up."

"It's more than that, Kale."

"And I want more," he challenged.

Ronnie sighed. "You're a soldier, Kale." She turned her face from his neck so she could look at him. Her dark eyes were molten, raw. "You will leave again. I don't know if I could do it, especially now." She looked at his face and then ran her thumb across the mangled flesh. Him getting hurt affected her way more than he'd ever realized, more than he'd ever expected.

His fingers raked through her hair and she closed her eyes. "It's my job, baby. It's who I am. It's my world, a world that I very much want you to be a part of."

Her eyes blinked open and she stared at him. She held his gaze for seconds, hours, hell, when she looked at him like that—like she was broken and she needed him to fix her—time stood still.

"You do now," she whispered, exposing her fears to him. It made her vulnerable, and it made her more fucking beautiful. "Until you don't anymore. Then where does that leave me?"

His arms wrapped tightly around her and he buried his face in her hair, kissing the top of her head, wishing like hell that this stubborn woman would hear him. "You don't get it, sweetheart. I've never wanted anyone the way I want you."

She leaned up on her elbow and he followed. "Relationships are hard, Kale. You don't know what you would be getting yourself into."

He saw the calm. A smile tugged on his lips . . . He was almost there. "You will have to walk me through it, but I'm a quick learner. Come on, this hearts and flowers shit won't be so bad, I promise."

She smirked.

"What's so funny?"

Her teeth tugged on her bottom lip, trying and failing to suppress a smile. "I brought you flowers."

Kale looked over at the bookcase. "Ah, you did, didn't you? What was that for? Get well sympathy bouquet?"

"No." She jabbed him in the ribs but she couldn't help laughing at his smart-ass comment. She got up, walked her sexy, naked body over to the bookcase, and grabbed the flowers.

"Damn, sweetheart, are you trying to kill me?" he asked as she walked back to him.

She stopped in front of him and flung a hand up on her hip. "Mind-fucking me again?"

"Baby, I don't need to mind-fuck you," he said, bouncing his eyebrows at her. "But seriously, sweetheart, my health is questionable right now and you strutting your sexy ass around my living room in nothing but your 'fuck me' heels is going to put me in an early grave."

"Shut the fuck up, soldier." She slammed the bouquet against his chest and he laughed.

"I knew I would get you to keep those on for me sometime."

Ronnie huffed and rolled her eyes, slipping out of her heels and climbing back on the couch next to him.

"Ah, I didn't mean for you to take them off . . ." Kale whined. He winked at her, then picked the card off the plastic stem and opened it.

I don't do flowers, remember? But I want more too. . . .

⁂

Kale looked at her and the smile that spread across his face was panty-dropping gorgeous and Ronnie actually blushed. "You want more?

She nodded and inched closer to him so that her body was pressed along his. The smile in his eyes was worth any heartache she was setting herself up for; she just hoped like hell that he was right, that he wouldn't break her heart.

"And you were going to make me sweat it out this whole time?" Kale asked, his smile still firmly in place, dimple and all.

"I didn't intend to. But then I saw your face and your leg and I just got swept away. I was just so happy that you were okay that—"

He pulled her down on top of him and kissed her. It was deep, his tongue slowly filling her mouth. She wrapped her hands around his neck and deepened the kiss even more, her body jolting back to life as his hands greedily trailed up and down her body.

"So more, huh?" he asked when he finally pulled up for air.

"If you're up for the challenge." God, she hoped he was really up for it. She was all-fucking-in now. No turning back.

"Baby, I was up for the challenge months ago," he whispered against her neck as he dotted quick chaste kisses down the side.

Ronnie tilted her neck to the side, wanting him to reach all the places her body was begging for. "Well, looks like I can tell Harold he won't be needing that new artist next week."

He pulled away and looked at her. "What are you talking about?"

"Today was my last day at the shop. I sold the house—"

"You're moving?" he interrupted.

"I was . . ."

He shifted slightly beneath her and she tried to adjust her weight so she wasn't pressing against his thigh but her attempts were short-lived as Kale's arms held her firmly in place. "Where to?"

"I hadn't figured that out yet."

"Good, you will move in here," he said, a sexy, lopsided smile breaking out across his scruffy cheeks. She could get used to that smile . . . but not every damn day, right?

"What? That's fucking crazy, Kale."

He shrugged. "Nah."

He was out of his mind. "Are you kidding me? That is the

stupidest idea I have ever heard." Although, she had to admit it was tempting . . .

Kale laughed, probably because her face was in shock. "Why? I'm sure we could come up with a good arrangement." He shifted under her again and she could clearly feel his body hardening against her. Her own blood flowed hot in her veins when she felt the tip of him tickling over her pooling warmth.

"Yeah, because the last arrangement turned out so well," she said sarcastically, trying to catch her breath.

His hand slipped up her bare back to her nape. His fingers toyed gently with the strands of hair, igniting goose bumps down her neck. His head leaned forward, kissing a path to her ear, making her all too sensitive skin tingle all over again. When he reached her ear, he nipped it gently, and then whispered, "I think it turned out great."

His arms molded around her, her body sinking onto him, fitting together like lock and key. She laughed to herself. She would never give another woman shit about wanting that tattoo ever again.

Ronnie looked into Kale's clear blue eyes—her very own Captain America—and smiled. "Yeah, I do too."

EPILOGUE

Ronnie stood at the edge of the bleachers, her nails pressing into the palms of her hands as her high heels sank into the soft ground of Cooper Field. The evening was starting to cool the thick Texas air, thankfully, because even in October the heat seemed to stick to her skin.

Never in a million years did Ronnie think she would have followed another soldier across the country from one duty station to another. But when Kale got promoted to first sergeant and received orders to report to Fort Hood, it only took her a single breath to know that she would follow him. Yeah, she'd made him sweat it out a little while she thought it over for a few days, but she hadn't needed to think it over. She was all in.

Kids were running around the field while other family members stood around talking anxiously and clinging onto their Welcome Home signs. The Honor Guard and the soldiers with the First Cavalry horses stood to the right of the field, waiting. They were all just waiting.

It had been six months since Kale left to take over command of Sapper Company, which was stationed in Iraq. It was hard at first for Ronnie to wrap her head around the idea that Kale was leaving again, and so soon after he came home injured from his last deployment. But as much as it killed her, as much as it scared the living shit out of her, seeing Kale so excited, seeing him so anxious to return to his job, gave her a sense of pride that she had never felt before. Sure, she knew it was going to suck having him gone, but if she wanted to be a part of his world, she was going to have to take the good with the bad.

"Attention, families, I have just received news that your soldiers have landed at the Robert Gray Army Airfield and will be bused here shortly," the division commander announced through the microphone attached to the podium in the middle of the field.

"About time." Ronnie sighed as a smile crept over her face and an annoying group of butterflies inhabited her chest. She shifted her weight nervously, causing her heels to sink farther into the ground. "He's home," she whispered.

The plane landed and the silence that smothered the air in the cabin evaporated. The guys started talking back and forth, their voices carrying loud conversations throughout the small space. They were finally home.

Being away from Ronnie for the last six months had been Kale's own personal hell. He'd never truly understood what it felt like to leave behind the woman you love, until now. It was a day in, day out heartache that felt like a piece of him was missing. He missed her with a fierceness that consumed his thoughts and overtook his dreams. The missions and his soldiers made the days move by quickly, but it was his nights that stretched on forever. The memory of her body curled next to him, her long hair spilling around his face, her soft moans—it haunted him. But not tonight; tonight he would hold her against him again. He would feel her for the first time in six months.

"First Sergeant?"

Kale snapped his head away from the window of the plane and toward the specialist that was hovering over his seat. "Yeah?"

"You all right there, First Sergeant?" the young guy said, not even trying to suppress his humor toward his distracted first sergeant.

"Yes, I'm fine. Why?" Kale said, twisting his hands inside the pockets of his ACU pants.

The kid looked down at where Kale's hands were stuffed in his pockets. He smiled again. "You just seem a little . . . er . . . nervous."

"Don't you have something you need to be doing, Frick?" Kale yanked his hands free and repositioned his patrol cap on top of his head. Frick laughed and stepped back from the seat. "Yes, First Sergeant."

Kale stood up in front of his seat and looked around at his guys. He had only known them for the last six months but he had formed bonds with them that most first sergeants couldn't pull off in more than a year's time, if ever. These were good guys, and they deserved the welcome home they were about to get. The plane came to a complete stop and the soldiers started cramming into the aisle, forming a tight line that led to the door of the plane. Once they were all outside, more lines formed to sign their weapons over to the armorer before they piled onto the four Bluebird buses that waited to take them to Cooper Field, to their families.

Kale sat on one of the buses and waited patiently, well, as patiently as possible, while the remainder of the single soldiers received their barracks keys and meal cards. He hoped like hell that they all had family here to welcome them home and take them out to a nice dinner and put them up in a good hotel, but he knew firsthand that wouldn't be the case. Unfortunately, not all of them had someone back home waiting on them. Kale never had, not until now.

Finally, the buses were loaded and once again the easy conversation among the men had shifted to silence. The tension in the bus was saturated with anticipation and excitement and nerves. Most of these guys had wives and kids they were coming home to, and the wait to see them was finally coming to an end.

The bus turned on Battalion and made the journey to Cooper Field. The road was closed to traffic for the welcome home celebration, and it was strange to see the post surrounding the road so still. It was like time was waiting on them.

As the field came into view, chants and cheers started ringing throughout the bus, igniting more excitement from the soldiers. Signs were held high while everyone was on their feet waving and smiling and trying to get the first glimpse of their soldier.

"All right, guys, you ready to see your families?" Kale shouted as the bus came to a complete stop in front of the field.

"Hooah!" The sound of the men shouting their response was deafening and the pride Kale felt at that moment had his chest tightening and his nerves spiraling out of control.

Kale stood up in the aisle and faced his soldiers. "All right, Sappers, let's do this!"

They all stood and hurried off the bus, quickly getting into formation behind the buses so they were still out of view of the field. Smiles were engraved on every single soldier's face, and Kale was no exception. His lips were tilted up so tight he felt it in his eyes. Once all the buses were cleared and the men were all in formation, the buses pulled away, revealing the soldiers to their families. Cheers erupted as they marched onto the field and the anticipation to be reunited with Ronnie damn near strangled him. He spotted her immediately. He had no doubt that he could find that woman blind. She was standing in front of the bleachers that were centered to the field, and her delicate hand was resting on her hip. Her long legs were covered in jeans that clung to her like a second skin. Her hair was down, and it seemed longer than before, tumbling over her shoulders, nearly covering her breasts. And her red heels—he knew she wouldn't let him down. She wasn't waving a sign, she wasn't hollering or cheering, she was just smiling—the real one, the vulnerable one that she reserved for rare occasions and they were all for him. The post commander had better hurry the hell up with his speech: Kale had a woman to see.

Ronnie scanned the field searching for Kale. The men blended together, forming a sea of tan-and–sage green digital camo. Their heads were covered in their caps and their hands were stretched behind their back at parade rest. Damn it. Where the hell was he? She had waited for this day for the last six months and now that he was right here, right in front of her, she was itching to see him. Her heart thudded against her chest and she had the urge to slip out of her heels and run onto the field and through the formation until she found him, just so she could see him.

And then it was like a magnetic force swept over her and her eyes fell on his. He was staring right at her. His smile was stretched across his freshly shaved cheeks, making that all too sexy dimple appear, and his blue eyes were clear and bright. His arms locked behind his back made his shoulders appear even broader. The material of his pants pulled against his thighs as he stood with them apart. God, seeing him but being unable to touch him was killing her.

He continued to watch her, a smile planted firmly in place. He winked at her and she felt a wave of heat brush across her cheeks. She knew what was running through his mind, because it was running through hers too.

The post commander stepped up to the podium. A silence fell across the crowd of families and the soldiers moved their attention to their general, but not Kale. He held her eyes like he was afraid he would lose sight of her if he didn't.

No words the commander spoke registered with Ronnie. She was too focused on the man that had commanded her attention since he walked into her tattoo shop, the man that made a deal with her on Valentine's Day, the man that fell hard for her and refused to give up on her, even when she was willing to give up on him. The man that loved more than she even knew possible and the man that cared more than she ever knew one could. He was a good man, he was a good soldier—he was hers.

"All right, families, go get your soldier." She heard the words echo through the microphone but before she could register them, everyone was running onto the field. Men were kissing their women, and scooping up their kids. There were laughter and tears, and above all excitement.

Ronnie stood frozen in place and watched as Kale slowly made his way to her, taking his time, teasing her as he crossed the field. His powerful gaze locked her in a trap, one that she wasn't interested in getting out of. It felt like time was moving in slow motion as he walked to her. He still had a slight limp to his step, but if anything it made him more appealing, especially to her.

Her heart wedged its way into her throat, making it hard for her to swallow. He was here and in just a few more steps, she would be in his arms.

Kale closed the last step between them, his lips no longer in his sexy grin, his chest pressing against her, her legs brushing against his thighs. They just stood there for a few moments, looking into each other's eyes, not reaching out and grabbing onto each other, just looking—putting the face to the memory that had been embedded in their minds, telling each other what no words could say.

Kale's eyes slowly left hers and trailed down her body, taking their time, over every line and curve. She felt the desire in his eyes burn through every inch of her body as he took her in. When his eyes finally made their way back to her face, a slow, lopsided grin lifted on his lips.

Ronnie smiled back. "Hey, soldier."

"Hey, baby." Kale wrapped a hand around her neck and pulled her to him, their lips crushing against each other's.

Warmth spread throughout her body as his tongue entered her mouth and explored her with a tenderness that consumed her. Her hand reached up and cupped the side of his cheek, her fingers brushing against the smooth ridge that formed his scar. Kale trailed his hand from her neck, down her spine, and rested it on the small of her back, pressing her tightly to him.

His lips moved harder over hers and a low moan rolled from his throat, vibrating against her lips. He pulled away all too quickly, resting his forehead against hers.

"God, I missed you," he said, his breath bouncing against her mouth.

"I missed you, too."

Kale smiled, pulled his head back, and cupped her chin in his hand. "I love you." He planted a quick kiss to her already tender lips, and then dropped to his knee.

Ronnie's heart stalled, her breath hitched, and her legs

wobbled beneath her. She knew what was coming and she didn't know how badly she wanted it until right then.

"So, sweetheart, what do you say about us making another little arrangement?"

Ronnie's pulse quickened and she swallowed hard. "Yeah, what do you have in mind?"

Kale reached inside his pocket, his hand in a tight fist when he pulled it out and placed it in front of him. He slowly rolled back his fingers, a diamond ring resting in his palm.

"How about forever?"

Read on for a special preview of
the next sexy contemporary romance in
Kelsie Leverich's Hard Feelings series,

FEEL THE RUSH

Available now from InterMix
wherever e-books are sold
and
available in March in trade paperback
from Signet Eclipse.

Meagan turned on the shower and waited for the water to heat up as she stripped out of her clothes. The day had taken an unexpected turn. Seeing Reed at the hospital was—a surprise. And the way he was with his soldier was adorable. It was like there was no sign of the company commander in him, just a buddy coming to see a buddy. She could imagine all of his men liked him and respected him for how involved he was with them. He was so relatable—not stuck up on some high horse with a rank power complex. No, he treated his soldier just like any other guy, and she admired that about him. Meagan had lived around soldiers her entire life, hell, she was raised by a soldier, so she knew a thing or two about a good leader when she saw one, and Reed—he was one of the good ones, but in a way like no other. He was so different. Whereas Kale took no shit and had a balls-to-the-wall mentality with his men, Reed seemed more laid-back, more compassionate, and more patient. And it didn't surprise her in the least. He was a big goofball wrapped up in a sexy package of solid masculine authority.

His silliness was what had attracted her to him—well, along with the fact that his entire body seemed to send shivers down her spine every time he came in close proximity of her. But when she pushed that silliness aside there was an intensity to him that she couldn't escape. It roped her in and tied her in knots, leaving her to wonder—what was shifting underneath all that carefree playfulness that wanted to claw its way to the surface? What layers of Reed had she yet to see?

"Hey, Meggy?" Eva said, knocking on the bathroom door.

Meagan cracked the door open and peeked her head out. "Yeah?"

"I'm going to the gym. I'll be back in a little bit."

"All righty, see you later," Meagan said before she shut the door.

She turned on her iPod, setting it down on the counter, and stepped into the shower, singing as she stood there, letting the water run over her. There was something about taking a shower at night that made everything better. Her mom always said it was washing the day away—not that she had a bad day to wash away, but old habits die hard. Meagan closed her eyes, enjoying the light spray of the shower hitting her skin. Her limbs instantly loosened and her muscles went slack, the blood slowing in her veins as she relaxed—maybe she should have taken a bath instead.

"Um, Meagan?" a deep voice said from the other room. Outside her bedroom maybe? The hall?

Crap.

Meagan stopped humming and froze. The warm water

did nothing against the chill that suddenly slid down her spine. She just stood there for a moment, listening.

After a few erratic heartbeats, Meagan turned off the water and grabbed the towel from the hook on the wall, wrapping it around her as she quickly went to the bathroom door and opened it just a crack. She'd heard someone, hadn't she? And she was pretty sure it sounded a lot like Reed. Oh gosh, if her imagination was starting to hear his voice when she wasn't asleep—yes, she had dreamed about him . . . once. Damn it, twice. But he was just so damn sexy, and unfortunately, every time she closed her eyes since she had seen him that first night, her mind—conscious or not—automatically went to him as she remembered the way his stomach and his thighs looked without clothes on. . . .

"Hello?" she called out, stepping into her bedroom. She didn't see anyone—or hear anyone, for that matter. Great, she really was imagining it. She needed to get laid, this finding-Mr.-Safe thing was starting to mess with her. If she didn't find Mr. Safe soon, she was going to have to invest in a new Mr. Dildo.

She pulled the towel tighter around her as it started slipping down her breasts and walked into the hall that led to the living room and kitchen. Still no one. See, if this were a horror film she would be Dumb Blonde Number One, going to investigate a voice she heard in the other room while she was showering in her empty apartment. *Smart, Meagan. Real smart,* she said to herself as she padded barefoot and wet down the hall.

When she stepped into the living room, her feet automatically shuffled a few steps back and she damn near dropped her towel. Luckily, all the muscles in her body seemed to go on high alert, stiffening like stone, including the muscles of her fingers that were now wrapped around the towel in a death grip. Reed was standing with his back to her, leaning over the kitchen counter. He was wearing a pair of black gym shorts that hung down past his knees and a light gray cut-off army PT shirt. And of course he had to look amazing in it.

After the shock of seeing him standing in her kitchen diminished, she cleared her throat. "Reed?" she asked, the sound of her voice causing him to spin around to face her. She clutched onto the towel that separated her naked body from Reed's stare, which was now locked on her like he had on X-ray vision goggles—and damn it, it was hot.

"Hey, Meagan." His eyes shifted over her and he dropped his arms to his side and licked his lips. Whether or not he did it knowingly, she didn't know, but the slow, subtle movement had Meagan's thighs pressing together. He might not remember her, but she sure as hell remembered him—especially her body. It was like the memory of him hovering over her left a physical imprint on her skin, and it was walking the line with torture. No matter how many sexy looks he sent her, or how many times that tongue of his reached out and swiped across his perfect lips, she was not going to go there again. He was Mr. Safe's arch nemesis—her plan's arch nemesis. He was anything but safe, she already knew that.

When she didn't say anything he continued. "Sorry. I didn't realize you were taking a shower. I was just writing you a note. I passed your roommate in the hall and she told me you were home and to walk on in. I'm sorry." His eyes squinted slightly, garnished with a flash of mischief. Yeah, his words might have said he was sorry, but the slight pull to the corners of his mouth paired with the intensity in his eyes said that he was anything but. The asshole was amused.

Meagan was sure her face was about ten different shades of red at that very moment. She had no doubt in her mind that Eva had given him the go-ahead to come in the apartment. The little tramp was plotting something, Meagan just knew it, and when Eva had something up her sleeve it never ended well.

Meagan didn't respond; she just looked at him, puzzled.

Reed smiled, that damn mouth of his perfectly crafted into what was now a cocky smirk that made Meagan want to shake her head in exasperation, yet at the same time it made her want to drop her towel and give him something to smirk about—but she wasn't that ballsy.

Reed reached around the counter and lifted a large brown paper bag. "You like Mexican food?"

He had brought Mexican food? Okay, first off, major brownie points scored right there, Mexican food was her favorite. And second, he was surprising her with dinner? Hmm.

"It just so happens that I love Mexican food." She started walking toward him, curious to see how much more this guy could get right. "What'd ya bring me?"

Reed's eyes were unashamed, slowly traveling down the length of her body as she got closer to him. She tightened her hold on the towel that was wrapped around her; it just barely closed completely. If she took too long of strides, he wouldn't need any X-ray vision.

She watched as his eyes, which seemed to be more liquid gold than brown at the moment, returned to hers. He swallowed a few times and wet his lips again. She was affecting him—she could tell, and she liked it. It gave her a sense of power that suddenly made her want to strut around the whole damn apartment in nothing more than the towel, just so his eyes could continue to warm her body from the inside out, just like they were at that very moment—but again, not that ballsy.

"Well, I didn't know what you liked, so I hoped for the best and bought the basics and my favorites. We got your chicken fajita quesadilla, a couple supreme tacos, and my personal favorite, the loaded loco burrito. I've got enough queso here to last us until next week and"—he walked around the counter and picked up a milk jug filled with a lime-colored liquid—"margaritas."

Meagan scrunched her nose at the jug in his hands and his persona instantly shifted. The intensity was gone, and his playfulness was back in full swing, and although Meagan was relieved to know that her body might stand a chance at being in the same room with him without feeling the need to take a walk down memory lane, she was also slightly disappointed. She shouldn't, but she liked the way he had looked at her moments ago. It'd been a while since a man looked at her like she was his favorite dessert.

"What? You don't like margaritas?" he asked when he

saw her face contorted into a disgusted scowl. He looked slightly wounded, like his puppy had just died or something, and Meagan couldn't help but laugh.

"Oh no, I love margaritas, but I'm really picky. I'm a tough critic when it comes to my margaritas, and that jug of juice you've got there, my friend, does *not* seem appealing."

"Okay, well, I was going to let you finish your shower in peace and leave this nice food here for you to enjoy by yourself." He grabbed the note he was writing off the counter and raised it for her to see. Sure enough, it said he was going to leave the food and head home since she was in the shower. "But now I want you to get your cute ass in there and change, because, quite frankly, you're very distracting in that towel, and then come back in here and I will wow you with my margarita-making abilities."

Cute ass? Distracting?

She smiled at him, an unexpected flutter pattering against her stomach, and turned on her heels, knowing good and well she shouldn't. She should just tell him to leave and go finish her shower—but she caved. "On the rocks with lots of salt," she said over her shoulder before she picked up the pace and trotted down the hall to her room.

Well, fuck. He didn't expect her to be in the shower when he walked into her house. And he sure as hell didn't expect her to come walking out of the hall looking surprised with her big, round eyes, her blond hair clinging to the side of her face and neck, and her body dripping wet from head to toe—but it was a sight he wouldn't mind seeing again.

He had wanted to surprise her—to thank her. He knew good and well that she shouldn't have called him after Brewer's surgery, and he definitely didn't expect to see her check up on him after her shift. She was going out of her way for him, and for his soldier, and that said a hell of a lot about her. Brewer didn't have anyone here, and a pretty face like Meagan checking in on him every now and again would be good for the kid—keep his spirits up.

"I hope you don't mind sitting on the floor, our stuff hasn't gotten here yet," Meagan said as she returned to the kitchen. She had her hair wrapped up in a towel, which was unusually adorable, and she was wearing a pair of shorts that put Daisy Duke's to shame, paired with a snug-fit plain black tank top.

There was still something about her that had his head swimming. His body responded to her, but hell, he was a man, he didn't think it was possible for any man to be near her without their dick getting a little rise from the way she looked when she scrunched her nose or twirled the tuft of hair at the nape of her neck. This woman was oozing with sex appeal that she didn't even realize she had. She was sweet, but in the way that made him feel like she could be anything but sweet, given the right opportunity, and he would most definitely like to give her that opportunity.

His mouth became moist, his lips parting slightly as he allowed himself to toy with the thoughts that entered his mind as his eyes traveled over her dulcet body again. She fidgeted with her fingernails and shifted her weight from side to side, waiting for his response—but he was enjoying taking the time to breathe her in, watching as she grew eager. "Nah, I don't mind at all," he finally said, deciding to put the poor woman out of her misery.

She threw a couple of pillows down on the floor. "Good."

"All right, I need you to taste this for me," he said, handing her a red Solo cup filled with his margarita. "And when you're done tasting it, you can give me a big fat thank-you followed by the words 'Reed, you're the best.' "

Meagan laughed. "Is that so?"

Cracking a smile, he nodded. "Yes. Now try it."

Her tongue flicked out and skimmed across a small section of the Solo cup, lapping up the salt before she pressed the rim of the cup to her lips and took a sip. Which was sexy as hell, and he was sure she didn't have a damn clue.

The instant she pulled the cup away, a smile broke out across her face. She was trying desperately not to, but it was a lost cause. Her full lips parted and her white teeth went on display as her lips turned up in a smile that reached all the way to her eyes. "Damn it, Reed," she said, shaking her head, apparently surprised, and sighed. "You're the best."

Reed clasped his hands together. "Ah, I knew you would love it. No woman can resist my margaritas."

She cocked her head to the side and lifted her blond eyebrows. "Oh, is that so?"

He looked at her and stumbled over his words. Fuck, that didn't sound good. He opened his mouth to say something. . . . What, he wasn't exactly sure—he just knew women were sensitive about that shit and he needed to try to divert the situation to a different direction. But before he could get a single sound out of his throat, she spoke up. "It's fine, Reed. You can put away the ghostly guilt look," she said as she pulled the towel down from around her head and ran her fingers through the damp blond waves.

His shoulders slumped and he grinned, grabbing the paper sack off the counter and bringing it in to their makeshift dining room where Meagan had retreated, sitting on one of the pillows she had thrown down. "So, what'll it be? Taco, burrito, or quesadilla?" he asked, sitting down next to her.

"Well, I'm usually a burrito girl, but since that's your favorite I will let you have it and I will take the taco."

"Nope, here"—he handed her the burrito wrapped in foil—"you have it."

She took it from him, crossed her legs Indian-style on the floor, and started opening the burrito. "You don't have to twist my arm when it comes to Mexican food and margaritas." She took a large bite, sour cream and cheese spilling out of her mouth.

Reed laughed; he loved a woman that could put away food like a grown-ass man. "Good?"

"Uh-huh," she mumbled and nodded her head, lifting her hands to cover her full mouth as she laughed. Reed was still watching her a few moments later when she swallowed, wiping her mouth off with a paper towel. "What?"

"Nothing."

"Well, you're looking at me like I just grew a second head, so spill."

Reed released a long, low sigh mixed with a deep chuckle. "I like watching you eat."

Meagan smiled knowingly, picking up her burrito, slowly bringing it to her lips, and bit off another impressive-size bite.

Reed blinked his eyes slowly and shook his head. This damn woman seemed to enjoy testing his self-control. "Tease," he admonished, but the word came out in a throaty laugh—and sounded more like a plea than a warning.

Meagan gave him smile around a mouthful, reaching out the burrito for him to take. "Want some?"

She didn't know how badly he wanted some, but not the fucking burrito.

"Nah, you seem to enjoy it."

She shrugged. "Suit yourself," she said before taking another bite.

Reed dug into one of the tacos. "So this roommate of yours, what's up with her? I kind of got the impression she wanted to twist my testicles off when I talked to her earlier."

Meagan erupted in a fit of laughter that was contagious. Her hand covered her mouth as her small body shook and her eyes disappeared beneath her lashes, and Reed couldn't help but join in. The sound of their combined laughter echoed through the empty apartment. Meagan lowered her head to her lap as her laughter tapered off. When she lifted it again she wiped the tears that had accumulated and sighed.

Reed had a pain in his ribs, the good kind that you only got on the rare occasions that you laughed so hard it hurt. He missed laughing like that, it had been a very long time since someone made him laugh that way, but now that he had, he welcomed it. "Something funny I should know about?" Reed asked, his eyes wide as he watched Meagan's face slowly return to its original color.

She sighed again and smiled. "She is a spitfire. You might need to watch out for her. She may be tiny but she is tough as nails and if you piss her off I have no doubt in my mind that she would, in fact, attempt to twist off your testicles."

"Well, fuck. What did I do to piss off the fire-breathing dragon?"

She pressed her lips together, suppressing another laugh as the corners of her mouth twitched. "She's not pissed, she wouldn't have let you in if she was. She's plotting."

"Plotting?"

Meagan rolled her eyes and shook her head. "Yes, just ignore her." She pushed the nearly demolished burrito aside and stretched her perfectly tanned legs out in front of her. Yes, self-control was something of his she seemed to push, knowingly or not.

"If you say so, sugar."

"There you go with the 'sugar' again."

"What? You don't like it when I call you 'sugar'?" He lowered his voice and made sure to let his thick Alabama accent stroke his words before they left his mouth. Why? Because he could tell she liked it—he could tell by the way her face heated up and her legs brushed together, and anything he could do to get that kind of reaction from her, he would do it.

A soft flush spread across her cheeks, only making her

look that much more beautiful. She didn't come across to him as someone who got embarrassed easily, but he was definitely doing the job nicely.

"It doesn't bother me either way," she said, meeting his eyes directly. There was that confidence he liked. Her face may say she was affected, but her eyes—they weren't going to tell him so easily, and that was okay, he liked a challenge. "I do like your accent though, where are you from?"

Yep, that Southern drawl hadn't let him down yet. "I'm from Birmingham. What about you, *sugar*?" He intentionally let the sound of the *r* fall short.

Meagan cocked her head, her mouth parting in a slight smile. "I'm from everywhere." She lifted her finger and pointed to herself. "Army brat."

"Oh, yeah? You been stationed here with your family before?"

She shook her head and picked up her drink. She pressed it to her mouth, brushing her bottom lip across the rim of the cup, and then she pulled her bottom lip into her mouth, sucking off the salt before she took a drink. Reed needed that bottom lip in his mouth. He wanted to lean in and pull it between his teeth, then suck on it until it was swollen, and if she kept doing little things like that he might just do it.

She lowered the cup from her mouth and paused. Her head tilted a little to the side, her eyebrows furrowing before she blinked and continued to set her cup down. Reed was pretty sure he had the hand-caught-in-the-cookie-jar expression on his face and she more than likely knew why.

"Nope, this is the first time I've ever been to Georgia," she said, letting him off the hook from his staring, which he couldn't seem to control.

"And what do you think so far?"

"Well, in the week I've been here, I haven't really seen much to gather an opinion. I mean, I like it just fine. It's beautiful here."

"Have you ever been white-water rafting? They just opened up an urban course here not too long ago."

"No, I've never been."

"Oh, I will take you sometime. It's a blast."

"Okay, that could possibly be fun."

Reed flinched. "Possibly? Oh, sugar, you just broke my heart a little."

Meagan rolled her big blue eyes at him, then pushed her bottom lip out in a pout, mocking him. "Do you need a Band-Aid?"

"Ouch, woman," he said, clutching his chest.

Her lips tightened into a line, and she scrunched her nose, causing her eyes to disappear behind her long lashes. "You just strike me as the type of guy who would take the boat over a waterfall or something equally as insane, just for kicks, and I don't know how much fun that would be."

Reed smiled, she had him there—that was exactly something he would do. "Nah, with you, sugar, I would take it easy. That is, unless you like it rough."

Her eyebrows darted to her hairline and her wide eyes stared at him incredulously.

Reed threw his head back and laughed; he liked this

woman. He liked making her blush and he liked shocking the hell out of her, even if he hadn't meant to that time. "Get your head out of the gutter, woman. I was talking about the courses. There are several different levels, and some are rougher than other."

"Uh-huh. Nice cover."

"Think what you think, but it's nice to know where your head keeps going."

Her mouth gaped open and she made a little noise that caused his dick to twitch beneath his shorts. It was going to be a long night.

Kelsie Leverich lives in Indiana with her husband, their two children, and their three pets. When she's not writing you can usually find her behind the chair at her salon or snuggling on the couch with her kiddos and a good book. She loves stories that can sweep you off your feet, make you fall in love, break your heart, and heal your soul.

CONNECT ONLINE

www.kelsieleverich.com